needle in the groove

jeff noon/needle in the groove

 Anchor

Transworld Publishers
61–63 Uxbridge Road, London W5 5SA
A division of The Random House Group Ltd

Random House Australia (PTY) Ltd
20 Alfred Street, Milsons Point, NSW 2061, Australia

Random House New Zealand Ltd
18 Poland Road, Glenfield, Auckland, New Zealand

Random House (PTY) Ltd
Endulini, 5a Jubilee Road, Parktown 2193, South Africa

Published by Anchor, a division of Transworld Publishers
First published in Great Britain by Anchor
10 9 8 7 6 5 4 3 2 1
Copyright © 1999 by Jeff Noon

A catalogue record for this book is available from the British Library

ISBN 1862 30091 7

Typeset in 9/14pt Helvetica Neue Extended Regular by Kestrel Data, Exeter, Devon
Printed by Clays Ltd, St Ives plc

Designed by Lucy Bennett

scratches and samples

mike and linder/julie

howard devoto/richard boon

james noon/helena at waterstone's/pat cadigan

jon savage, for the books *time travel* and *england's dreaming*

piccadilly records/pelicanneck records

and most of all, thanks to cp lee

for the book of *shake, rattle and rain*

and the expert knowledge

rhythms

autechre/derek bailey/dj premier/king tubby

microstoria/evan parker/plastikman/pole

the smiths/sonic youth research/david toop

mix process

main body of work written in *analogue flowtext*

occasional use of *iambic digitalis*

dubs created using the *cobralingus filtering system*

dedicated to

$$C_6H_{12}O_6 \rightarrow 2CH_3CH_2OH + 2CO_2$$
and
Bm(+9)/D/A/E9/C#m(sus4)/E/F#///

glamography

the 4 glamorous men
1957 *ready steady skiffle!*
1959 *live at the 2spot*
the glamourboys
1963 *postergirls*
1965 *embrace you*
1968 *swirl*
the glamour
1970 *damaged goods*
1973 *tainted vein*
1977 *unexploded blonde* (unreleased)
the figs
1977 *skull*
1979 *flesh*
1981 *vapour*
glam damage
2002 *scorched out for love*
2003 *vibegeist*

one

scorched out for love

door code

the nightclub / a stonecold zombie with a look of shock on its face, the kind that happens when nocturnals get caught in the daylight / check that feeling / something about turned-off neon always does it for me, turns on the sadness, gets me thinking about where all the shine goes to / like it should've been raining, like it should've always been raining

what the hell

just this guy, you know, standing alone on ian curtis boulevard / sunday morning frozen, just gone nine / and even the moon has been left behind by the night, so careless, looking like a stain of bleach / like a close-up photo of how my head is feeling / oh please, I could do with some doghair right now / something wet to get the heart in tune, to keep my finger from shaking on the door buzzer / until this low-pitch squawk gets back to me

—who is it?

—I'm here to see donna

—who is it?

—it's elliot, look . . .

—who is it?

oh shit, the door's got nasty bouncer attitude /
I only met this donna last night and I'm pretty
sure she never mentioned a password

—who is it?

—shut the fuck up will yer, I'm thinking

—who is it?

I press my lips closer to the grille

—the bass player

sticky stuff

the door slides open, smooth as yer like /
and I have maybe five seconds to get myself and
the big case through before it closes again /
closes like a bad-breath mouth around me /
some kinda foyer, shuttered cloakroom to the
left, ticket booth to the right / suddenly warm,
like the building has a pulsebeat / and no one
around so I walk ahead, through into blank
space

club zuum / the dancefloor, shining away into
the distance / heat-shivering

and dirty / with my shoes sticking to the
spillage so much, feels like I can carry on walking,
right up the walls, make out like a fly for the day /
around the circle of the floor, where a couple of
old ladies are cleaning up the plastic glasses,
the cans, the swill, the vomit, the debris / I give
the bomb squad a wave, and they look up and
smile, and wave back, like a mirage / the club has
that glazed ozone feel / molecules of evaporated
sweat and perfume / the thousand-and-one

come-ons still lingering, sticky ghosts of young desperate sex

—where's the studio? I shout over

the women point me towards some steps / down / where a lone stiletto lies discarded, as though cinderella has turned sluttish / a regular trash palace / along a corridor now / deserted / past offices all empty of life / maybe I got the wrong day or something

holy shit / what am I doing here? somebody tell me

just tracking down the traces / the sizzle and the traces of a stranger's smile

when this big, old domestic cat saunters out of one of the offices / a mangy, battle-scarred affair, all black and tattered fur / the flea magnet looks at me, like I'm a fool to even be here / and then waddles off down the corridor, flicking its tail like it owns the world

well what the hell / I follow / into another doorway

some fat guy, standing near a kitchen counter, eating a breakfast burger

—what the fuck do you want?

—the studio?

—downstairs! down the fuckin' stairs!

hey, nice people / I walk back into the corridor, thinking it's maybe time to leave / no, really / when I see the cat again, sitting on its backside right next to a door / a wooden door this one, looks like a broom cupboard / open it / and there you go, more stairs, leading further downwards / into darkness / I look around for a light switch, find one / but it doesn't work / of course it doesn't

this is getting stupid

the old cat's looking at me / one eye is glued together with a clog of scum / the other's giving me this real voodoo manic stare

ok, cat / let's get to it

holding the case behind me, I follow the creature downwards / feeling for each step in turn / musty, cloying air / the damp on the walls meets the sweat on my skin / the drink being squeezed out of me / and down, and further down

some other kind of door at the bottom / no answer to my knocking / louder now, and still nothing / and then swing the door open, letting the cat nip through my legs / I follow it through, into a recording suite / empty / a glass partition shows a room beyond / darkness / near dark-ness / people / another door leads to them / I push it open

just standing there, holding the bass / looking through

heavy on the download

oh yeah, I play the bass / the bass plays me / the four-stringed, thick-bellied electrified monster, you know, the one that eats all other noises alive

and I've gone walking down these four strings most every hour of every day, of every year and every busted heartbeat, just trying to get along to where the last riff kisses the dark / the subsonic groove, we call it

dub culture / midnight's vibration / something to reach for

some throat, some bottom, some neck and some deep clutch of riverpulse / gets you hot just strapping yourself into the thing / and the more you play, the hotter it gets, the slicker the slide / and all for nothing much because none of the songs you discover, ever come anywhere near to what you hear in your dreams

and I guess all that follows is about me taking a chance on the journey of the bass / and finally getting to reach the end of it / the end of the last

tune, and what I find down there, in the grooves
of the soul / and how come the music is always
that one step beyond all the love you play it
with / and how the bass ain't got four strings at all
   just when you think you're getting the grip of it
   how it's got these other strings, invisible like /
below the low, and deepcore / you gotta dive
down underload to get a finger on them / and
watch yourself doing it, watch yourself
   those strings can pull you under, believe me
   ah shit / believe me please

the glamour

a room of smoke / with tiny lights glistening, red and green / instrument control patterns / figures in the gloom

—hey up

somebody speaks / turns on a lamp / the scene gets focused

three of them / two women, one man, seems like / and there I am, all eyes upon me

—you made it then?

it's the voice / the smile / the one I've been following since last night / donna, that's all I know / just this girl who came up to me after the gig, said she liked what I was doing with the beat and that she had a thing of her own going on, and maybe I could put some flavour to it

—just about, I answer

and who wouldn't / who wouldn't follow / round about nineteen, twenty at the most / check the style / the twisted nest of the hair-do / the tight, capped tee-shirt / the tattoo on her arm, a playing card / and the dark dazzle of the skin / oh yeah, she's black / kinda black / with the deep pool of the eyes / the big bold mouth, smeared with purple / all things about her filled to the brim / and so easy with the smile, it was there even when it wasn't / but now it was, most definitely / and it's aimed right at me

    —what yer looking at? she asks

    —you

    —who the fuck's this? says the other woman

    —tommy, isn't it? asks donna

ah shit, this girl is doing me down

    —elliot

    —come on then, elliot / don't be shy

laughter

    —yeah, fuck you as well

and then step right into it / the studio, cramped to the walls with stuff / amps and mics and recording equipment / one entire wall, floor to ceiling, is vinyl records / the whole shebang wreathed in smoke / no outlet / ok, I've had a few thousand spliffs here and there, all down the line / but this is serious fog stew / gets me dizzy, just by breathing

    now the woman who's invited me, this donna, she's leaning against an amp, smoking one of these rollmop constructions / smiles through the hit, and I smile right back when she holds out the joint to me

    —no ta

—what? she says / you don't want any?

—not right now

—what's wrong with yer?

—tell yer what / I wouldn't mind a drink

now that gets her funny somehow / gets her looking around at the other two, with a feeling I can't catch a hold of

—got this, she says

handing me a bottle of juice, like orange juice

—a drink I'm after

—it's sunday morning, she says

—yeah / and you're at the dope already

—fuck me, says the other woman / we got one here

—that you have / and what of it?

donna does the intros

the second woman, the one who just spoke up / introduced as the dj, given the name jody / she's sitting lonely behind a turntable deck, examining the grooves of a twelve-inch single / I get to see her frown one more time, that's it / except / oh but the way she's running her fingers over the vinyl surface, as though tracing / searching / buried treasure

now the guy / he's lying on a small couchbed affair, holding a pair of drumsticks / just tapping out some off-planet rhythm of his own / like, erm, the drummer I guess

donna nods towards him

—and this is 2spot, she says

2spot / well there yer go / neat black shirt, buttoned high to the neck / pale skin, drawn along the cheeks / high, dense sweep of blond hair greased back into a flattop quiff / sideburns sharpened, right down the groove of the bones / toughnut style, but something a little bit fluffed about him, you know / a touch of the flowers / too sweet a smell, and a softness around him / like never a day's work has been done / and maybe I've seen him around, maybe playing the drums somewhere, I don't know / whatever, something coded passes / just in the brief nod he gives me / just that

and then donna points out the cat, curled atop an amplifier

—and this is gallagher, she says

—noel, or liam?

—paul, she says / and that's the whole crew

meanwhile, the smoke's really getting at me, bringing back stuff I don't really need / so I take a swig of the juice offered / just to cool the throat of memories / and then donna says

—glam damage

—yer what?

—yeah, what do you think of that, as a name?

—well / I can see the glamour

looking at mad jody as I say this / and then at donna

—and I can see the damage

the singer smiles deeply at the drummer / and then turns to jody

—there you go / he loves it / I told you so / I told you it was a good name

now this jody woman, she looks up at me, right at me / not a trace of expression

—you're late, she says / supposed to be here at nine

—it's what? I reply / twenty past?

—how would it be, if you turned up twenty minutes late / for a gig / how would that be?

—I got lost

—how would it be if you got lost?

—fuckin' passwords and all that

—you get lost, on the way to a gig? would that be good?

—that wouldn't happen / fuckin' hell / what's wrong with yer?

—yeah, come on jody, says donna / give him a chance

—you can fuck off as well

—oh, says jody / the guy's got problems

—I'm getting pissed off, that's all

so this jody stands up then / and for the first time I realise just what a specimen she is / a touch older than the other two, almost my age / but weird with it / I mean, there's weird and weird, right / but jody was off the edge of normal and right along some / nothing to do with how she dressed, because that was scruff central, with a touch of couldn't-give-a-monkey's-tutu hippie shit / but her face, her whole manner, every last vein spoke of jitter, of flex, of what the fuck / body pinched shut, and so thin, the skin stretched taut over wire / black hair scraped to fit the skull, knife-edge whisper / and two of the coldest eyes that ever did view the world, I swear / they were eyes detuned, right through zero, and into the minus

reminds me of a bathroom mirror I once knew, the one I had to veil / turn to the wall / the peeling silver skin on the back of it / and that too, eventually, I could not dare approach

—you been here before? she asks

—what, down here?

—the zuum club?

—no

—you don't like dance music?

—dance music, that's what you do?

—kinda

—kinda?

—the next step, you know what I'm saying?

—fine / the next step / whatever

—how old are you?

—twenty-four

—twenty-four, and you don't like dance music?

—ah, been off the scene a little / you know, out of it

—oh yeah, how far?

—what?

—how fuckin' far have you been out?

—look / maybe I should go / eh?

—you backing out? says donna

—just wanna know what the score is, that's all / I mean, you want a bass player / I am a bass player / I play the fuckin' bass

—five or six bands, he's in, says donna / right this moment

—five, six or seven bands, by the way

—nothing serious though, says donna / pub bands

—ooh, he's played in bands before, says jody, with a darkside sneer / now us, you see, we ain't played in any bands but this / this is a pure band

—no bands but this? how many gigs?

—no gigs

—together how long?

—together three months

—oh fuck me, a buncha babies / this really isn't what I'm after, my friends

—just listen to us, says donna / that's all we want

I mean, tell me please, what would you do / come on, just to get the thing over and done and outa there / get myself some air, some proper juice inside me / some lube / some breakfast at the very least / so I give the nod, and

—right, says jody / scorched out for love / let's do it

the drummer gets up from the lounger / this is a guy who hasn't said one word to me / not one single word the whole time, not even to the other two / he gets up and just kinda slides into position behind the drumkit, sticks at the ready

well then, here we are / down to the wire

—crack it open, says jody

and the drummer hits the skin / down hard

scorched out for love, original mix

down hard / creeping patterns / snares and rimshots, like a fall of rain / the held crackle of a cymbal / bass drum coming on the third beat / caught in a loop / rhythm dancer / drums, and nothing but, until donna dares to sing this down-time lament

waiting for the world to learn
the contours of your skin
I wonder what colours you'll turn
when the world burns

I was expecting some impassioned outburst / but her voice has a calmness to it / degrees of control, almost on the edge of becoming some-thing else / she sounds lost, uncaring / stretching out the words / bruised with hidden knowledge

drums and voice / a flat chant

jody comes in on the second verse / working a shimmer from the turntables / fingers dragging plastic, holding it / releasing / holding / releasing / building a noise / a caress of stolen notes surrounding the song, tightly bound / by the end of the verse she's managed to twist the feel entirely / making it tremble, succumb

and then explode / she must've hit a switch somewhere / turned on some pre-recorded kaleidoscope / this sudden howl from stretched strings / vinyl pops and screeches / machines crying and scratching fire, right up the nerve scale / until the sheer blade of it gets stuck tight in the darkness, shoots right back at me / into the chorus, with donna allowing a slice of emotion to cut through

that's the way of the world my friend
when a world comes to an end
we throw it all away
to start again

and down / further down

not slow, but like poison to the beat / jody juggles another disc onto the decks / incisions of bootleg guitar, choked off / real familiar, scraped from the grooves like magic / it's the deep-down motherlode, it really is / a ton of work to be done, for sure / but donna's singing, all that slow tragic honey dripping out, word by word, dropped between the beats / and the dj's crazy tactics on the samples and scratches / I mean, if this is three months' work, I'm amazed

but mostly, oh most of all, the drumming / this

2spot guy can play / you hear him now, splicing the third verse open with scattershot blasts / and down / down flat funky / holding / holding / making some splinter, making some blow

deep jesus in the groove / have I been waiting for this / like all my life, seems that way / through all the cul-de-sac affairs, the dead-end gigs / the slimeball singers and the junkyard songs / the lousy-arse contracts / all the drugs and the booze and the subhuman blues / all the thrash-happy merchants of the traps and the kit / all that shit / at last, at last / some proper goddamn loving on the skins at last, for me to drop the bass injection

listen to it / off-kilter cuts from the shine of a cymbal / alive with sparks / and a criminal tension that jody's scratching caught, and threw back / down in the cellar, on the other side of town, just this tripwire of sound / twisted space / and all the flavours of noise / gliding away

and throughout the whole song / that stupid cat / gallagher his name / that scruffball just slept on / top of the amp, like soaking up the music, every last ounce

one last funky fuck flow-down falling
and gone
crackle of silence

a deeper high

—what do you think? says donna

—we were slow, says jody

—I like it, I say

you know, playing it cool / but donna's got this big smile for me, which was ok getting on the end of / 2spot meanwhile is combing his hair / doing the whole thing in three practised sweeps, one on each side, and then the top, setting the quiff back in place / not a touch of sweat upon him, like the guy just sauntered out of the fridge

—where did yer get those guitars from? I ask / the buzzcocks?

—yeah, says jody / sampled them / you know the tune?

—just about / yeah, what yer did, it's good / it's a good song

she looks at me for a second or two / the usual hard fire stare / and says

—you got something for us?

—let's have a look

right then / here we go / let's show these

people some / except that all of a sudden I'm nervous / nervous / now there's a first since way back / but the way they play together, both ragged and tight / I'm gonna have to ride this one fine / real fine

I open the big case, take out the creature / fender precision / old style / flip the strap over my neck, attach the end to the little clip / feel it swinging / I mean, this bass just hangs wicked / like a bomb, like a cloud / sure, some weight to it / but distributed just so, around the centre of gravity / always feels like I'm floating / and plugging it in, is like plugging myself in / they have this old bruiser of a bass amp, valve-driven / the sweet, sweet buzz of the power surge as I jack the flex / the thing comes alive in my hands

christ, I'm coming over all heavy metal / when all I'm saying is that I have a real love affair with that moment, the plugging in

gettin' engaged to the sun, I call it

—I'm gonna record this, ok? says jody

—fine by me

she does the business in the control room / works some switches, whatever / comes straight back out and we get the thing moving

with me coming in on the second verse, just behind the first turntable scratch / making it deep, making it weird / all the roads I've been down / the usual bag of tricks / stretching it out, trying to keep the feeling alive / against the odds, because yer know this stuff ain't my natural language / not at all / I play too solid, it kills it / play too loose, it's a mess / and the sweat on the strings, making the fingers slide / and the smoke in the room, and the smoke in the heart

until something weird happens, almost by accident / with all the instruments and the singing falling into a bad shape, a loose hole / I'm trying to get out of it, back into rhythm / until I'm wondering, shit, what is this / it's a tightening, a coil / with the whole song on the everywhere edge of falling to pieces / but just about glued

and shit me, but jody was right / it is kinda pure / pure and cleansed, well almost, on the subsonic soul

angels in the rhythm

grab the feeling, my fingers / turn it into a riff

and just go off floating

because something happens, just sometimes / and when it happens / just sometimes, just sometimes / you grab that flow, and go / come out the other side of the song, covered in sweat, shaking with it / let the strings go slack on the last note / and then breathe out, first time in minutes gone by, lost in the traces and the feedback buzz of the holy bass mother

even the cat is up and purring some / smiling like alice just walked in

2spot thumps the drum, says

—nice playing, bassman

the first words I ever heard him say

—I think so, says donna

—that do yer? I say to jody

—very clever, she says

—ah, what's fuckin' with this woman?

—yeah jody, says donna / we've tried too many already

—sure, says 2spot / he's the best yet

—it ain't funky enough, says jody

—yeah well, I answer / where I come from . . .

—what?

—we don't have no funk

—no funk?

—damn right / small northern town, what do you think / last in the queue when god handed out the funk / hey look, I did what I could

now they're all looking at me / straight down the line

—let's make him funky, says donna

jody looks at her, shakes her head / and then walks through into the control room

—what's going on? I ask

no really, I mean what is this / they're gonna make me funky?

—you'll see, says donna

jody comes back out in seconds / and I swear there's almost a smile on her face / almost / and the 2spot guy, back on the couch, he's got this trace of a grin / and gallagher the cat, smiling away / and donna of course, smiling for everyone

like I'm on the end of the biggest joke of all time

and then the music starts / top volume

drums in the playback / listen

scorched out for love, soft remix

back in the drum-play / listen to it / 2spot shots of a down-hard creeping pattern / snares in the rainfall, caught in a dancer's downtime rhythm-loop lament / where all the cymbals sing

waiting for the bass to skin, the contours
of the world

the voice-edge of donna, degrees of bruise-control / lost on the hidden sound chant of knowledge, now stretching passion burst / jody, working a plastic drag / kaleidoscopic shimmer from the fingers / holding, releasing / stolen noise caressing the song of tremble notes

I wonder what colours you'll burn, when
the bass returns

tightly twisted strings explode / scratching / succumb to the sudden switch howl, a hit from slow darkness / turntable nerve fire / blade the scale / stuck in the shoots

*that's the way of the bass my friend, when
the bass flows to an end*

and down / and down flat funky
tragic splice tactics, on the samples and the
slices
the pops and vinyl screeches / along the decks
of poison, scraped from the bootleg / choked
off the disc / incisions of strange groove, made
of mad magic / guitar heart crying out, rhythm's
injection / the motherloading bass honey, dripping
deep, and word by word crazy

dissolve it all away, to float the song again

splinters / the off-kilter cuts from the bass /
down in the amplifier, on the other side of town /
tripwire noise-glide, release into chorus / all the
patterns of flow / catching the flavours
deep jesus of music / and the drumfall of the
groove, catching
the final
silence of crackle

the damage

—what the fuck was that?

—the remix, says donna

—the what / get the fuck out of here

—what's wrong, says jody / you never done a remix before?

—no I have not / all that techzak shit

—this ain't techzak

—right, and you were, what? fifteen seconds at the mixing desk / I mean, the whole song's been messed with

—yeah, totally

well, almost / everything was there, more or less, but changed into something else, moved around, broken, made new / even the words of the song had been shifted around / and most of all, the bass / the hometown bass, given some nasty, given some disco / it's me playing, I'm sure it is / but sexy, somehow / shit, it was almost bootsy collins

—fuck! it's not possible

—show him, jody, says 2spot from the couch

—come on then

she leads us all into the control room / the big desk there / loads of add-ons, just taped into position / a real sound lab / jody presses a button / and the music pops out / recorded material, handed right over into my hands

—what's this?

—what's it look like? says donna

—I don't fuckin' know / a globe?

—it doesn't look like a globe, says jody / it is a globe / what's inside it?

I'm holding this thing / no disc, no tape, no cassette, no cd-rom / just this fuckin' sphere, the size of a golf ball / plastic, at least I think it's plastic / made of a clear, slightly malleable material, and inside

—it's some kind of liquid, I answer

—sure it is / take a look

donna turns on a desklight, and I hold the thing up to the beam / the globe is filled with a sky-blue liquid, quite thick it seems, quite sluggish, with darker strands of colour here and there, caught suspended / the light burns through it / tropical / oh yeah, there's some heat coming off it / and a nice weight to it, a certain heft belied by the contents, as though it contained some extra substance / a secret cargo

—this is what we played? I say

—that's what we played, says donna

—but how?

—who the fuck cares, says jody / the club zuum label have exclusive rights to the first usage

—we're testing it, says donna

—it's called wave recording, says 2spot

—liquid music, says donna

—liquid music, jesus / so how does the remix work?

—all I did, says jody / is give it a little shake

—a shake?

—tiniest possible shake / just a soft mix, you know, nice and easy does it

—what happens, says donna / is that some of the elements have a stronger chemical bond

—a lock, says jody / against the flow

—so there's always a reminder of the music, says donna

—but the more you shake it, says jody / the deeper the mix

—it's the way out, says 2spot

so I'm looking at him, and then at jody, and then at donna / not knowing what to think, feeling dizzy with the thing / and then looking at the globe in my palm

—shake it up, says donna / go on, see what happens

so yeah, I give it a shake

and slowly, the darker strands, they swim gently around into new shapes, new patterns

—harder, says jody / all the way, all the fuckin' way!

harder, shaking harder / watching through the beam as the liquid breaks down / becomes jelly / veined with new arrangements / new meanings / and never stop shaking until all the veins are broken

—look at that now, says donna / you just done your first ever remix

—oh yeah, says jody / it's dj fuck face, on the decks

—bad and busted, says donna

—scorched out for dub, says 2spot

the globe lies warm in my hands, settled at last / and when jody plays it back for me

ah shit

scorched out for dub, elliot's bad and busted remix

    the creeping two-shot spots of a flow-down /
drumfall and the rim of skin-beat, in a snare-
dancer's downtime rhythm-loop explode lament /
where all the rain cymbals sing / the contours
of the voice, waiting for the bass to steal, the
sliced and crazy feel / shots of the lost / the
hidden sound chant knowledge caught and
twisted, now stretching guitar burst / a drag from
the fingers / holding, releasing / noise caressing
the blade-song / I wonder what colours you'll
burn, when the bass returns / bruise of crackle-
pattern, vinyl screech-pop of string / the sudden
switch howl scatter of rhythm / a hit from
stretched plastic, down in the darkness / cellar
blast of turntable nerve fire / singing, that's the
way of the bass my friend when the bass flows to
end / and down / and further down and down /
and down flat, along the decks of slow noise
poison, scraped from every last bootleg / on the
other side of town / incisions of chorus, made of

mad magic / amplifies the heart crying out, injection dance / cuts of motherloading bass honey, off-kilter dripping deep, and then word by funky word, passion splinters the tragic splice tactics / on the caught samples singing it all away / all the tripwire scratching kaleidoglide of a strange groove / deep jesus bass of music, catching the shimmer / the final crackle of silence / holding, releasing / dissolving

blues in a rented room

I have a little place on state 808 street / right beside some old, abandoned industrial estate / from my window, when I get home later that day, I can see the sky darkening around the lonely factories / at last, I get some drink inside me / sit myself down on the tiny, unmade bed / take out the globe

donna's given me this / around the diameter, a band of white paper, indented / and scrawled upon it, *scorched out for love – remix 24*, and the date / mind you, I must've shaken it up some, just in the car / so, huh, remix 25 now, isn't it / christ / what's the point of numbering them / just a slip, the thing falls to the floor, the music changes already

ok, the globe is sliced barely flat, one end, so you can stand it up / like this, on a small bedside table / and opposite the flatness, some kind of tiny slide affair / valve system / I can't see a way to open it up, not easy / no doubt this is where they get the liquid inside / but hold it upside down, like this, nothing drips out / and just turning it over, like this, and the liquid moves around, gently, softly

remix 26

I don't know what to do, whether to join or not / sure, the singer's got the twilight charms, and the drummer plays a coming home rhythm / and they're all being paid a decent wage by the club zuum label / sure, they're a proper band, and that's the problem / I've done the proper band thing, and look where that ended up / and that jody woman doesn't even like me / and do I really need to be around all those drugs again / all those demons one more time?

I've reduced my life to the booze and the fags / that's love enough / sure it is / ah, I'm ok with the pub bands / the five, six or seven nowhere for ever pubrock bands

hours later, I wake up / alcohol all over me

that fuckin' tune / playing around the skull

Bass Instruction Manual

To wake the strings so tightly bound, let slide
The finger's nub along the neck from fret
To fret; from bridge to nut, the tones collide
And sound the joyous air! And yet, and yet . . .

a genuine punk love song, maybe

so yeah / hi there / the name's elliot / elliot hill / no nicknames, nothing stupid / I'm yer man, the guy / wretched little soul, granted, and fulla shit, but it's my shit, yer know what I'm saying, hand-crafted / here's a story

sunday oct 2, 1977, the last night of the electric circus

the circus was the first great punk club in manchester / every sunday for a year, in the sinking estates of collyhurst, all the bands came to play / the place was the focus / the out-of-town centre of the swirl / the coming together, the making space / cold, and grimy, and dark and caked with years of sweat and love / good love, bad love, all kinds of love / and now the council were closing it down / a fire hazard, or some such excuse / two nights would seal it, the last saturday and sunday of the city's explosion / fused / the buzzcocks were top of the bill, sparkers of the flame / and all the manchester bands playing over the weekend magazine / the fall / warsaw / cooper clarke / the drones / the worst / the figs / john the postman / the negatives / the prefects / many more, never to be remembered

and the fans / place them up there with the players / the wall to wall mess of noise / move in close on just two of the people in that place, that night / nobody famous / a man, and a woman / call them that, a boy and a girl really / teenagers / punks / with the uniform and the attitude / carefully collected / but the boy was on the scene, trying to be anyway / knew some of the bands, just to talk to / and for this special time, he'd invited the girl along / it was only their third date

and by the end of the gig, the circus was wrecked, and swimming

and the kids, the two in question, something got them going that night, something wicked / something got changed inside them, set loose / something to do with the time and the place / something more to do with the buzzcocks / just this super-fast whine of guitar and twine, dragging a tide in their blood

white hot sulphursonic

their names are dave and sue / just ordinary names / nothing special

except / that afterwards, around the back of the building, in the carpark, in the creaking, cold car / they did it / yer know, did the dirty / now that doesn't sound romantic at all, but it was to them / it was, it was / mean down and dreadful, but lovely / but lovely like bending down to scrape some dogshit off your shoe and finding a diamond stuck there, right in the smelly, sticky lump of it

and that, as they say, was my mum and dad, doing it / dave and sue / and what they were doing, the dirty, that was me being made

so they say / and that the music made them do it

and if you believe that, believe anything

but you know, I've done the maths / yeah, born in 1978, the month of june / could be true, could be half true, could be a pile of arse / most definitely, knowing the dad, a pile of the most supreme arse currently available / like he wasn't even there at all / I'll bet

but you know / like who the fuck cares, really

a child of the buzzcocks?

oh sure / it's as good a way to be got, if you've gotta be got at all

down the vein

this old and crooked structure on the stranger side of town / right there on ludus drive / the house has a name, *tainted vein*, quaintly poker-burnt into wood / and there they live, all together / jody, donna and 2spot

glam damage house

turns out it belongs to the drummer / likewise this van we rode around in, and all the equipment / his mum, now get this / 2spot's mum lives in london, from where she owns and runs the entire club zuum network / oh yeah, the guy's being kept

mind you, there's nothing too fancy about the place / rehearsal room down in the cellar / as dark and as damp as you could want / and nothing flash, no liquid music machines / just the amps, the instruments, the cheapo decks and samplers, a reconditioned portastudio

we make music down there, all the week / and I have to say, away from the club, the band is even better / we make a noise like I've never known, just this one great stripped-raw channel of searching out / for the first time in years, I'm actually playing something / all the smalltown dregs of flair get magnified and yer know what, I can't help falling in love with the whole idea of being brilliant / to be myself at last, lost in the rhythm / oh yeah, severe romantic arse shit, like yer don't see any more

and then, some nights after a rehearsal, I'll stay over / sleeping downstairs on the settee / upstairs, the three rooms / a pile of household junk in one / jody alone in another / 2spot and donna in the last

oh yeah, 2spot and donna / a thing going on

it's got me disappointed, that's a fact / got me surprised as well, because you don't see much evidence / passion, I mean / even in that first week for instance, 2spot just took off one day, just rode the van out of there

—hang on, I say / I thought we were rehearsing

—he'll be back, says donna / he always comes back

and she shrugs, like that's it / and that is it, I suppose / because the next morning back he comes, 2spot, his face all clouded / and they kiss / it's an ok kiss / there's nothing wrong with that kiss / except that / ah, maybe they keep it all for the bedroom

don't even think about it

but you know, great times / really / getting up late for breakfast, jody making it / a pretty good cook, at the old bacon and eggs level / the mangy black cat will sit there patiently, waiting for the rind / oh yeah, gallagher's in there, home in the van like another piece of equipment / bloody weird / a stray, just turned up one day, became the group mascot / actually, the thing isn't black at all, but the dirtiest, darkest grey you can imagine, striped with soot / looking like a prowl of smoke

and then donna will come down, hair all over the place and sometimes just dressed in a wrap-around affair, or even just a shirt, one of 2spot's fancy numbers

ah / now then / the tingle / like a tune being played / oh yeah, desire / hot blood desire / like a crazy bad tune I haven't dared put my fingers on / not for a long time

with donna catching me glancing / and is that smile really for me?

whatever

great days / great mornings / and then, usually about an hour after everybody else, 2spot will come down / always dressed up to the edges, no matter what / with the suit, and the pressed shirt / all that hair in perfect position / and giving off this smell, this air of flowers he has about him / no tie, nothing like that, just all the buttons done up to the neck, and right down to the cuffs / looking

good, so good / and there's me in the semi-
casual sportswear

jesus / what a bunch

as soon as 2spot appears, that's when the day
really begins / jody drags us all down to the cellar
/ even the cat's invited, always just sitting there
on top of the amp, watching us play

ok, how it happens

we always start off with some background that
jody prepares / vast, dense landscapes, made
out of samples / all the stolen moments of stolen
songs, broken open / jammed up solid into new
shapes / then she gives us the title, hands the
lyrics to donna / donna starts to sing, just sliding
the words into the mix, any old how / searching
for the melody / then I'll come in on the bass,
counterpoint and wraparound / somehow or
other, we find a groove

and when 2spot hits the skinkit / only then
does the track get funky, really funky

only then

he has this style all of his own, and one time
he explains it to me / puts this record on, doesn't
he / some obscure dance number, forcing me to
listen to the rhythm track alone

—you see now, he says / how all the per-
cussion parts are kept separate / just that cymbal
there, now the bass drum, now the snare?

—that's easy, I say / it's a machine / hot-wired

—yeah, and that's what I am

this is how he works it out, telling me that in dance music it's like they take a drumkit to pieces / and then they just use the pieces one at a time

and that's how he plays, for real / like a precision machine / piece by piece by piece by scattered piece / coming together

like a goddamn funky as fuck precision per-cussion machine

—how long yer been playing?

and then he tells me to back off

—back off, bassman / no more questions

he was like that, about himself

no more questions

and the days all fly away / every last note of every last jam recorded and played back, and the tracks dissected for treasure / and no matter how great they sound, always jody will say

—not yet, not yet

—let's get something out, jody, I say / do some gigs / make some proper money out of this

—not yet, not yet / not till we're ready

—I'm living off the savings, jody / down to the dust

—come and move in with us, says donna / we get more work done

—there's no room

—sure there is, she says / spare room, we can clear it

—no

I'm there near every day anyway / and every sunday down the club zuum studio / transferring what we've got onto the liquid system / hearing it float away different every time

aquamatics / hydrophonics / wave-sonic technology

donna explains it, halfway explains it / knowledge caught in particles, suspended in a charged medium / analogue heaven

and all the best mixes saved onto master tape as well and I know we have to do it, capture the evidence / but really, I just want all my bass-lines to be liquefied / turned to mush / changed to bass-lines I would never play / bass-lines nobody would ever play, could ever play / and there's the love of it / the unheard beauty of the tunes, dissolved anew / and drop by drop, the liquid is teaching me / fluid techniques / learning to lose the finger's grip on the beloved riff / getting a hold of that funky stuff feeling / because how does the song go?

throwing it all away, to start again

yeah, that's the one

because music was never meant to be captured anyway / music is a wind-borne expression, like love / it's here and then it's gone

here and gone and here and gone and here and gone

we capture it, that's just a chance meeting
and I guess this newfangled gizmo is the best
yet to map that vanishing / a liquid map, to chart
the notes as they pop and sizzle from the fingers
or the throat, and then fade like smiles, away
ah yeah / they should have such a device for
love / they really should

this kid, made out of wire

thinking back now / to where it really starts

for the ninth birthday, I receive a package through the post / mystery present, no return address / flat cardboard box, twelve centimetres square / inside, no note, no nothing, just some metal / that's right, metal, check it out / a bound circle of metal / a curled, sleeping snake

unloose it gently

and let it spring open / quivering life / silver vibrations dazzling the eye / it can't be caught, the metal can't be caught, once loosed / living thing, metal thing / silver thing and snake thing / shaking thing / a tiny bolt affair on one end, and the other end just disappearing, into sharp-cut air

—what is it? I ask the dad

—bloody hell, he says / somebody's sent you a guitar string, let's see that

—who sent it? says the mam

—some mysterious person, says the dad / look, it's a G string

—don't be dirty, says the mam

—don't be daft / a G string for a bass guitar

now the dad, he ain't got a fleck of music inside him, not even the smell of a tune, so I don't know how he knows that / and anyway, what a lousy present to send a kid / so throw it away, and end of story / except

for the tenth birthday I receive another parcel, the same thing inside

—the D string, says the dad

I don't know where he's getting all these letters from / I really don't

—you see, he says / it's slightly thicker than the first

he'd got the first wire out of hiding, just to compare / and here's me thinking it was thrown away

—who's sending them? asks the mam

—how would I know, says the dad

for the eleventh birthday, metal / quivering

—the A string, says the dad

each string fatter than the last

—means they're getting deeper, says the dad / never forget that, lad / the fatter the string, the deeper the sound

—who's sending them? asks the mam

—you're sending them, I say to the dad / anybody knows that

—no, the dad says / look at the package, a london postmark

—who do we know in london? asks the mam

—next birthday, says the dad / I just bet the lad gets the E string, and that'll be the set

and what do you know, for the twelfth birthday, nothing / no parcel, no metal, no quivering thing to catch a hold of / can't say I was arsed really, just bits of wire / but you know, a sense of something not quite done / not quite finished

the dad rolls in from the pub that night, and says

—nothing yet, lad?

—nothing yet, I answer

—ah well, then / maybe next year, eh?

for the thirteenth birthday, zero / no metal / we all pretend not to notice / and by this time, the dad has turned a bit cold on me / and me on him / getting older, yer know / the both of us

for the fourteenth birthday / listen now / two days before the event, I go to the only shop in town that sells musical instruments / lousy little shop, all dark and musty / where I ask the guy for an E string for the bass guitar

—an E string, you want? he says / but we only sell them in sets

—I don't want the set, I say / I've got the other three already

he looks at me, the old codger, like I've crawled out of the hole in one of them old spanish guitars he's got strung up behind him

—well now, he says / let's see what we can do

and he rummages through this drawer, pulls out a plastic bag / inside a full set of bass strings / he takes one out, separates it from the rest / lays it on the counter

—I shouldn't be doing this, he says / ruined a set, haven't I / well go on then, take it

—how much? I ask

—how much yer got? he asks

I've brought the savings along for this / the paper-round money

—that'll do it, he says

—all this, just for one string?

—that's the price

and what do you know / for the fourteenth birthday I receive a package / just the one package, mind / just the one / sent it to myself, didn't I?

trouble is, the dad's not even home to see it arrive / he's lost his job this year, and spends most of his time down the boozer / most of the morning recovering / most of the day getting ready to get himself lost again

—who's sending them? says the mam / and oh look, it's got a different postmark / right from this town / how strange

—they could've moved, I say / hiding the game

—yeah, there's that / they could've moved

so we get all four of the strings out / lay them

all out, side by side at full stretch / the G, the D, the A, and the E / weird little word, spells out nothing

    —it's a shame, says the mam / you ain't got an instrument to put them on

    —I'll get one, I say

    —oh elliot / wherever from?

    —I'll get one

the score

—and did you? asks donna

—what?

—get one?

—a bass guitar / sure I did

—what, they sent you one? this person?

we're all gathered around the kitchen table, eating takeaway food

—no / no, they didn't send me one / no they didn't / bought one myself, didn't I / left school early, nothing to show for it / just to get a job, just to make the money / drop by drop of the money, just to get this cheapo thing down the shops / with a little practice amp and everything / and the first thing I did, yer know what?

—take the strings off? says 2spot

—take the crappy strings off the bass / and put the other ones on / the good ones

—the birthday strings? asks donna

—yeah, the birthday strings

—so who taught you to play? asks jody

—me / the small, lonely back-bedroom of the heart

—and why not the fourth, I wonder?

—the fourth?

—just three strings they sent you / strange

—just to get me started, I suppose

—and who sent them anyway? asks 2spot

—it was the dad, wasn't it / the stupid bastard / of course it was

—from london?

—sure / ordering them special / before he got too pissed to care

and to celebrate the fact, I take another slug of wine / watching as the usual gear comes out / donna rolling up, and jody supplying, and 2spot combing his hair / and I'm right in the middle of my usual excuses, when jody says

—come on, man / relax a little

—I am relaxed

—you're all fucked up / go on, take a drag

—I'm ok

—ah, what a downer

—I just don't, that's all

—well then, I just do

—yeah, I can see that

—what's that mean?

—nothing much

—he's gettin' to me / he's gettin' to me

—jody, says donna / he doesn't, right / just leave it at that

—well he needs to

—maybe he's done enough already, says 2spot

that gets them quiet, even jody / and I'm thinking, ok, let's get this out of the way

—yeah / yeah I did / and now I don't

—what was it, asks donna / like serious

—oh yeah, serious / detox city

—I knew it, says 2spot / I just knew it

—two years now, clean

—fuckin' hell, says jody / he boozes more than all of us

—that's clean / believe me, that is clean

—ah, he's really pissing me off now / he's making out that nobody should

—I'm not saying that

—well go on then

—what?

—say it then

—say what?

—go on / say to me now, loud and clear / that anybody can do anything

and all I can do is look at her

—ah fuck / you're a cold-hearted bugger, no contest

yeah / no contest, jody / absolutely

ok, here's the drug score / the house score

bottom of the pile there's me, holding it down with the liquor and nicotine / and then donna and 2spot, both of them safe and easy / strictly leisure-time enjoyment and no big deal / and then jody / ah shit, I don't even like thinking about it / the stuff it brings back / taking drugs because what else is there, except for life's frictions / and I don't know what she's taking, and I wouldn't mind so much, but she's hiding it away somewhere / oh yeah, she's a bedroom specialist / strictly private, and all we get is the outcome / the good mood, bad mood / good mood, bad mood / all that / top of the roller-coaster, bottom of the dive / and then some

the vein's bad-arse outlaw song / the one that never stops asking for more

and of course, it's a danger to me, being anywhere near that song again / but here I am, falling in love after ages of not daring to, who would have thought it / with the house, with the band, with the music

—yer know, I say to them / this is a big thing for me, joining the band

—you betcha, mr clean arse, says jody

but the singer and the drummer give me the nod / like they get the picture

funnily enough, out of all of them it's the drummer I feel most drawn towards / intrigued by / just the secrets around the guy / the dark penumbra / the way he gets that faraway look in his eye, and then just takes off in search of whatever

and the only thing that gets us anywhere near to close / the music, the music

and maybe if I'd been anywhere capable, I would've seen the trouble / right there / right there in the music that dragged us together

and oh, by the way / I got all those drug scores completely wrong

so badly fucking wrong

a deeper groove

the only time 2spot will really open up, is talking about the records / you should see the collection he's got, all the styles, all the periods / the man's into things I never even heard before / from the latest, most twisted and strange, right back to the raw and petrified / mind you, he's real tight about anyone playing them, touching them even, without him being there / but when the rare mood takes over, just sometimes he'll invite me up to the bedroom / he keeps all the best ones up there / and the best sound system in the house

for myself, I've never had much interest in going out too far, nor back too far / so I'm always after hearing the old favourites, just at top volume yer know, and with the special bass that 2spot's amp can render / he'll go along with this, right enough / pointing hidden details out, telling me stories about the musicians involved and who they were influenced by, things like that / expert knowledge / he knew more than someone his age should know / where was he getting it from / what was missing from his life, he had to fill it with all these records?

come clean / I like being up in the bedroom, just because, well, it's donna's bedroom as well, you know what I'm saying / there's stuff in here / female stuff / all over the dresser and the floor, and strewn all over the crumpled bedsheets / oh yeah, female stuff / things / fancies / you know, stuff / like concentrated essence / way beyond

the music, the music . . .

sometimes 2spot will take me on a journey / a way back, through tune after tune, track after track, seeking the source / usually we'd start with a dance record / like a techzak monstrosity / these are best because they use the samples / he'll play me this one item, highlight the sample for me, and then play the record it originally came from / from there, he'll show the history of that one particular beat, that one particular feel, usually all the way back to the blues

—that's where it all comes from, he says / from out of the blues

there are so many journeys to go on, from so many starting points, towards so many goals / all the world of music opening up for me / all the ways to make a noise, a tune / all the secrets, locked in the grooves / and it's during one of these explorations that 2spot finally reveals a little of himself to me, a little of his life

this is how

one time we happen back to this weird-sounding music, all rattle and clatter and bang

—what the fuck is that? I ask

—that's skiffle, 2spot says back / you've never heard of skiffle music?

—kinda

—kinda?

—tell me

and that starts him off

—skiffle / the 1950s / it's the beginning of british pop music / the first real teenage music, came out of american folk and trad jazz / the white-trash version of black music / played at speed with a rocking beat / kinda like a british rockabilly / check it out

yeah, check it

thick guitar chords, blocked out simple / the spick and span of high, tinny riffs / hypnotic bass throb / the monster teeth rasp of something weird being scratched at

—what the hell's that noise?

—a washboard

—a what?

—keep listening

the vocals that sing, loud and harsh, of a night on the town gone bad

johnny o johnny o
johnny o' palaver
down the piccadilly square
pulled out a blade on a roughneck shade
sliced him good and fair
ohh
he sliced him good and fair

2spot shows me the sleeve / it's a long-playing record, vinyl / sealed tightly in cellophane

—I never play them, he says / just record them / straight to cd / too valuable / it's too valuable to play

johnny o johnny o
johnny o' palaver
now they're shaving his hair
long time a singing, soon come a swinging
high in the hangman's snare
ohh
high in the hangman's snare

—how much is it worth?

—it's nothing to do with money / but to me / valuable to me

the cover / a black-and-white photograph / just these young guys, on a stretch of wasteland / playing their instruments / the 4 glamorous men perform *ready steady skiffle!*

—you see the bass there? says 2spot, pointing to the cover

—is that the bass? just a box?

—tea-chest bass / they made them themselves / it's like a punk thing / diy music / a tea-chest, a broom handle, some string

—jesus / really?

—yer can't really get a tune out of it, just a rhythm / anyone could play it, that's the point / but good sound, huh / what do you think?

—I'm not sure

—listen to that! you hear that guitar?

—I hear it

—imagine, eh, getting down to that / down to that level

I'm looking at the cover again

—they don't look much like men, I say

—what's that?

—the 4 glamorous men / I'm saying, they don't look like men / too young / too young to be men / and not that glamorous, come to that

—that's my grandad

he's pointing to one of the musicians

—you're kidding / this here?

—that's him

—he played the guitar? you never said

—saying it now, aren't I / twenty years old, he was / this is where it starts

—bloody hell

—listen to him / go on, just listen

I look up at 2spot / I'm thinking he must be kidding, really, but the way he's listening to the music, so intently, so passionately / and then look back at the sleeve, studying the figure pointed out / just a bloke, a young bloke that's all, could be anyone / turn the sleeve over / the album was produced in 1957 / there's a track-listing, and a line-up / the guitar is being played by somebody called danny axle / I look back at 2spot / he's still distant into the music, and it suddenly comes to me that I don't even know this kid's name / he's my drummer, sharer of the rhythm, and I don't know his real name / he's 2spot, the 2spot guy

turn the sleeve back over / this young man, standing on a pile of rocks, holding the big, semi-acoustic guitar so proudly / I'm searching for resemblances / looking so closely, I almost miss the most obvious one / the hair / the bloody haircuts / they all have them, all four of them, and here's 2spot right next to me, the very same / the quiff, the sideburns, the grease, everything

—what you laughing at? he asks

—nothing / well, the hair

—he gave me this cut, when I was a kid / taught me all the techniques / see?

he's handing me a jar of something from the bedside table / dixie blossom, it's called / inside, this goo, smells of lavender / lavender and something else / oh yeah / petroleum / lavender and petrol

—you put this on your hair?

—same stuff elvis used

he combs it into place, just to show me / and the smell, the flowery smell he carries around / this is where it comes from / real strong, this close up

—you got any more records like this one?

—more skiffle?

—more with your grandad playing?

he turns to look at me / it's a strange look, almost fearful / I'm thinking maybe I've asked for too much, gone too far / he's on the edge of putting the records away, turning off the system / happened so many times before, cut by his moods / and then he suddenly relaxes, as though catching hold of something, at last

—sure / got loads / he made seven albums altogether

—seven?

—official releases

he's searching through the collection, pulling albums out, one by one

—there's a couple of bootlegs as well / and some unreleased stuff / I've got everything

—they have bootlegs, of skiffle?

—he wasn't just skiffle / he moved on / here you go

he hands me another six albums, to the one I'm already holding / seven, altogether / the first two are by the 4 glamorous men / and the second of these really hits me / it's called *live at the 2spot*

—your name? I say

—the 2spot was a club in manchester / long gone now

the cover shows the group standing outside a dingy-looking building / the club sign is a painted two of hearts

—so why call yourself that?

—I didn't / grandad gave me the name / keep going

the next three albums are by the glamourboys, all from the sixties

—it's the same basic group, says 2spot / a couple of changes, but very much his band / he would never stand still, didn't know how to

and the last two albums by the glamour, from the early seventies / and I'm hit by the connec- tions / the glamour names, and our name

—he was always on the far edge of making it big, says 2spot / the glamour was his best shot / like to hear some?

that question / I don't know, it seems that all my life in some strange way has been hanging around for this moment / it's nothing really, just two young men, and a smelly cat by the way, sitting on a floor-level, unmade bed, surrounded by women's underwear and the stench of hair gel, and listening to records together

—I'll play you some glamourboys first, he says / they were his pop band / 1965

he finds a diy cd from the collection, slips it into the machine, presses play / and the single, jittery strand of a guitar comes along, a web for the vocals

I was too young to know
how to fall in love with love
but I cried my heart out over you
and all the lonely tears
fall down in secret places
when I cry my heart out over you

—this is him singing? I ask
—that's him
—sounds like the beatles
—yeah, well / you really didn't have much choice back then, about how to sound / check the sleeve

further clues / the album's called *embrace you*
the glamourboys embrace you

a moody, shadowed portrait, and there he is / danny axle, the quiff brushed forward and down into a fringe / no more grease, and strangely, he now looks a lot more like his grandson

—anyway, that's the beat stuff, says 2spot

he presses a button to eject the music, suddenly impatient / picks out another cd

—now this is 1968 / *swirl*, it's called

ok / from the album of the same name / all coloured beats and reverb up the arse and back / psychedelic mind-warp / with the requisite special effects, and words I can barely hear, from a million miles away

> *the clocks go blind*
> *the days unwind*
> *in the town of swirl*
> *and all the jokes*
> *are told in smoke*
> *in the funny little town of swirl*

it's a nursery rhyme, sung by a fool / a gentle fool, locked in a small room down the corridor from where all the guitar players get to go crazy

and just as I'm getting into it, 2spot clicks it to a standstill / replaces it

—now this is the glamour / final album / the real thing / the best

it's like he can't keep up with the feelings

but such a change this time / like a half-remembered dance / I don't know where I am any more / songs of wanting and loss / songs of crazy

—bloody hell, 2spot / he went through some changes

—that's what people did, before punk / all the music, yer know / all the music, there for the taking

all the music, so dark and ravishing / so sweetly taken

what the light considers
the dark of moon delivers
the sun that burns on midnight's turn
devours and spits and shivers

oh, whatever the words can mean, the man can sing them / there's a slow-motion soul to the voice, like the heart being squeezed, reluctantly, out of the mouth / and the lyrics made out of fragments, tangled images, episodes from a dream / through the craziness, a fall of sadness / a fall of pop sadness, played on a cheap saxophone / also, certain elements in there, certain moments now passing that our band have picked up on / in a sense, 2spot is taking me on another journey / he's showing me the roots of our music / the source

—it's a concept album, says 2spot

—about drugs, is it / sounds like

—don't make fun of him / please

—I'm not / so what's the story?

he shrugs / nothing doing / just handing me the sleeve / the album's called *tainted vein*, and there yer go, I was right / drugs / released in

1973 / and years later, giving us the house name /
so much coming from so long ago

the glamour, down to a solo / drums, bass,
guitar, vocals, keyboards, even the plastic saxophone, all played by the one guy / and here he
is, getting older with every release / floppy hair
now, a slight wave to it, a slightly dirtier blond /
strangest of all, he's wearing eye-shadow /
imagine that, a grandad with painted eyes / but
it's 1973, isn't it / glam rock / how old would he be
/ mid thirties, looks like / a bit too old for the game,
maybe / and I keep calling him grandad, taking the
cue from 2spot / his name is never mentioned

danny / danny axle

I look at 2spot / he's looking back at me / intent
stone-blue eyes, desperate, I think, for me to like
the album

—he's playing the drums on this?

—oh yeah / he taught me how to play / taught
me everything / but you like it, right?

—he's very talented / playing all these instruments, I mean

this seems to satisfy / 2spot relaxes a little

—what happened to him?

—he . . .

—what?

—he gave up / he tried once more, recording
some stuff / but by then the whole punk thing had
started / I don't know / he didn't like it

—what / he felt left behind?

—no / more than that / betrayed, I suppose / yeah, betrayed / you know, manchester in the late sixties, a lot of the clubs were closed down by the police / fear of drugs, and all that / there weren't many groups around then, and no real places to hear music / and my grandad, he always felt he'd kept the spirit alive / the spirit of the city's music / and then the kids turned against him

—so this is the last recording?

—yeah / the glamour / the last real thing / and now it's all mine

—what do you mean, all yours?

—the music, he left it for me / everything

—you mean, he's . . .

you mean he's dead / but I can't complete the thought / and so we listen in silence for a while / as this broken voice sings faraway songs

—he made this music, says 2spot / it'll be here for ever

for some reason, it feels like a secret being shared

—well, now I know where glam damage come from

—oh yeah, the name / all the way from there

—not just the name / but maybe why you're such a good player

—what's that supposed to mean?

and right there, just like that / all the closeness draining from his eyes

—you know / it must run in the family / I mean, does your father . . .

—what?

—music / the music . . .

—fuck off

—jesus, I'm just asking

thinking at first, maybe he's upset I made out his talent came down to him / like a gift, rather than hard graft / but then . . .

—you little fuck / what do you know?

. . . realising / I've never heard him swear before / and it's more than that, much more

—2spot . . .

—get out of here / get out of my fuckin' bed-room

degrees of pain, burning the face / the nerves set loose

—what's wrong / tell me . . .

—get out!

—I'm out / I'm out

christ, what was all that about / like I'd snapped a string, middle of a riff / the guy was stretched tight / way too tight

and he never played me records / not ever, after that

not ever

freeze and scorch

but yer know / great days, great days

fuck it / I just gotta believe that, no matter / no matter how cruel it all turned out in the end

not long after this incident with 2spot's record collection, we're down the club zuum studio one time, getting mad at ourselves / playing the *scorched out for love* tune, over and over / this is gonna be the first single, we all know that, and we've played it a thousand times already, recorded it every which way / stretched it, wrecked it, kicked it up the butt, twin-decked it / shoved the whole thing in the blender, to let the liquid mix do its thing

and I'm really feeling the bass these days / these few weeks with the damage, getting myself connected / jacked into something sweet, at long last / makes me really want to get out there, show the world how these four strings can get to mean so much

but still / jody won't give the word

november of the year, we're shivering through

the song / donna's voice freezes as it comes out of her mouth, each note sparkling / and the rattle of her tambourine, like a ringing of crystals / the club's heater has packed up, real bad / so we have a little two-bar electric fire / might as well be a photograph of heat stuck on the wall / none of us wants to be here except for jody of course, and she's in a real crazy mood / fuelled up and shouting at us all the time / the mad fucker process

it's all about changing how you play, to let the wave take you / you know that moment, that moment

when the brittle edge of donna's singing

we throw it all away

collapses into panic / just this schizoid swamp-fest of cracked samples, wildcat deck-scratches, crazy bass pulsations and 2spot's mutant beats / the rhythm turns into jelly, disintegrating completely / pure noise, and you're left thinking, how the fuck can people dance to this / the moment stretches, and then, and then, and then, out of the nowhere of it all, starts this bass lick / this really fine melodic fragment, deep in the chaos / gradually the other instruments pick it up, finding themselves again, building it, just waiting for that moment when

bang

jody hits a new sample, scratched live from the

vinyl / a real buzzcocking splinter of a thing / hits
the eardrums like shrapnel

donna does one line / pure black in the soul

and then start again

and we all hit the sharpness / head on and
hardcore / with the drum, bass, word and groove
/ scorched out / all the way

and the drummer, the singer and the bass
player, all turn to stare at the dj girl / as she takes
the globe from the machine, gives it the remix
shake / ah, you should see her these days, it's like
she knows the precise movements to make

plays it back

so loud / like a sunburst from the speaker
cabs, almost sets fire to the studio / as the dj
closes her eyes for a second or two / listens close
/ nods her head once or twice / opens up, and
says something / says it softly

—what was that? we ask

and the dj says

—fine / we're ready

E A D G

you hear that?

and now, we're ready

a week later, I pack my few things together /
stick them in the car / move in the house

don't even think about it

so easy, there's even no rent to pay / 2spot
gives it free, like he gives it to donna and jody / all
courtesy of his mum and the club zuum account
/ jesus, the kid's being pampered

and mostly, it's a pile of nothing that I bring
around / only the smallest package really counts,
and I'm not sure why

just these four antique bass strings, all tangled
up together / the knotted loop of metal / all the
teenage lustre gone from them / all the quiver and
the spark / and the playfulness, played right out of
them

but so what / so what the lustre, the quiver, the
spark and the play?

been carrying them, haven't I

oh yeah / been carrying them

powdering

my first night in the *tainted vein* coincides with one of 2spot's mystery excursions / we never play without the drummer, which means that jody disappears down into the cellar, working alone on textures / and you know what that leaves?

all evening long, leaves the singer and the bassist, getting well out of it at the big old curry-stained kitchen table / we have one bottle of wine, two bottles of wine, enough fags to last all week, the same amount of prime grass for donna / fat cat gallagher's perched on the table top / I swear, this is the most stoned feline in the known universe, what with all this passive smoking it keeps on doing / so no wonder it wobbles and slinks and keeps on falling off things / and donna laughs at me for saying such things / which is strange, and good, and mixed with the wine and all, well / yer know

we talk and we talk

about music, of course, other people's and our own / and our plans for the band / and the house and my doubts about moving in / and about how donna first joined the band, meeting jody at a record fair / oh, loads of stuff

—you always sang, donna? I ask

—no / well / only a little / I was at college before

—doing what?

—computers / yeah / programming, all that / ambitious, still am / I even had a job lined up, for when I left / but then / I got waylaid, I guess

—go on

—that record fair I mentioned / I found this copy of marvin's *here my dear*, you know that one?

—marvin gaye / no, never heard it

—it's his divorce album / amazing stuff / not really songs, just these incredible atmospheres that he sings on top of / anyway, so I'm standing there, looking at the sleeve, when I heard a voice beside me / you like that one? it says / and I say, yeah, never seen it on vinyl before / and the voice says, here, let me buy it for you / and she did, and it wasn't cheap / collector's edition

—and this was jody?

—this was jody / I ended up back at her flat / just this scruffy dump round the corner / and we got drunk together, listening to marvin sing / and then I started singing along, or trying to / jody picks up on this / said she had a song of her own

—which one?

—oh, one we don't do any more / said she was looking for a singer, just to test the melody out / so she says / just to see if it works / and well . . .

—it worked?

—never heard anything like it / never / except for marvin of course

—so that's when the band started?

—no / I was still at college then / we swapped numbers / didn't hear from her for a year, nearly / then a call, just from nowhere, saying she was ready to go now / ready to launch, and did I want in / ok, by that time I'd just started my first job, so I don't know why I went round to see her, I really don't / and by then she'd moved into this house

—oh, right

—oh right what?

—that's when you met 2spot?

donna nods, looks away / takes another drag of cigarette / another slug of wine / it was the first mention all evening, of the drummer's name

and all the time, from the cellar, the sound of twin-deck acrobatics making the floor shake

another song, being stretched from nowhere

—you all set for tomorrow? asks donna, bringing herself back to me

tomorrow, saturday / down the zuum / when jody plays *scorched out*, first time ever

—what if it clears the floor? I ask

—jody will explode, I suppose / and we'll have to duck

donna pours me another wine / and another / and another / so many, I'm getting the melt on, the good thing that booze does to the soul / and all the things that donna's been saying / opening up / it's making a tune in my head / making me want to reach out, to touch her arm / it's been a while, such a long while, since I . . .

the tattoo there, the two of hearts, pulsing on her skin

it's been so long, since I . . .

2spot's mark

stop / stop it / stop it now

—do you have a girlfriend?

—what?

what's she asking me?

—easy question / do you have a girlfriend?

—no

—no?

—I had a wife

—a what?

—you know, a wife

—you're married?

—like / for two seconds / well, we still are / not divorced / not yet

—what happened, the drugs was it?

—the drugs / oh / just a part of it

—bloody hell, you've done a lot / for twenty-four, I mean

—whatever / I was only nineteen, when it happened / too young

—my age

—what / oh / yeah / anyway I was in this band / you know the tulips?

—you were in the tulips?

—yeah

—but / like they've had albums out and everything / in the charts and all that

—sure they have / but that was after I'd left

—so what happened / musical differences?

—not quite / you know the singer?

—with the tulips? yeah, gabriella, right / I've seen her on the tele

—well . . .

—what / oh come on / you were married to gabriella?

—still am / mad, isn't it?

—but / but she's / she's . . .

—oh yeah / beautiful / absolutely / and I never did work out what she saw in me / but yer know, we were in love / madly in love / met and married just like that / just a crazy thing

—this is what, before the band started?

—yeah / we more or less started the tulips off / and they were good / a great band / sure, just your usual rock bollocks, but yer know / bloody good at it / and gabbs was a great presence / star quality / I really thought I was gonna make it / the big leap

—but it's difficult, right, going out with some-one in the band?

—you think so?

—I think so

—ok / I'd been into the drugs since whenever / just falling into it / falling in love with what they did to me, and where they took me / and gabby was having problems with that, fair enough / and the band was getting courted by the labels, big time

—what, they dumped you?

—ah / there was an incident

—an incident?

—you know, an incident / never mind what / I made a fool of them one night / right at a gig / I was seriously adrift / and there were maybe four or five, half-a-dozen label scouts in the audience / special gig, yer know

—fuck / but that's no reason to get rid of you, is it?

—by that time . . .

—what?

—it was obvious to all concerned, what was happening / with gabbs and the guitarist / you know the lead guitarist?

—oh yeah / good-looking guy

—and they were writing songs together / all these fucking love songs

—jesus

—anyway, I wasn't sticking around / and I've never done anything since / nothing good

—till now?

—till now / and I wouldn't mind, but the tulips / they're still using my bass-lines

and I down a glass in one / feeling good, all that out of the way / with donna looking straight at me, a deep sadness playing in her eyes

—what's wrong? I ask

—it's jody I'm thinking about / yer know, she's hooked up badly

—I guessed that

—well sometimes / sometimes I wanna leave / because it's gonna get worse, right?

—unless she stops

—how? I mean, how did you?

—get nasty on yerself, don't you / one day

—just like that?

—that's the start

—and now, you never would / the needle, I mean / that's what you did, isn't it?

—that's what I did

—and now you never would?

—I can't / I can't answer that / anyway, why do yer want to know?

—about the needle?

—about the girlfriend

—curious / why you're so lonely

—lonely / yeah well / I'm getting over it, I guess

—and anyway / I've been thinking about us

—us?

—2spot and me

—ah / you got a problem?

—you know something, elliot?

—tell me

—you remind me of him

—of 2spot?

—you not noticed that / that lonely thing / that's why I picked you out

—you picked me?

—yeah, at the gig that time / that first night, playing the bass / I thought you could, yer know, get on with him / because he doesn't have friends, not really / male friends / not at all

—and that's it / that's all yer want?

oh god / the way / the way she's looking at me / and looking away

—so / where does he go then? I ask / when he takes off like today?

—don't know

—he doesn't tell you?

donna shrugs / she's knifing out two lines of coke / and it makes me shake, just seeing it

—isn't that strange, donna / I mean, with 2spot

/ why not / why not tell you / I mean, for instance,
what's his real name?

—2spot's name? axle, isn't it?

—his first name

—I don't know

—you don't know his first name?

another shrug / as she rolls up the money / and
then

—sometimes . . .

—yeah?

—I think he's got somebody else / you know,
another love

—another woman?

hanging onto this now / hanging on

—a woman / no / another group, silly / now that
would be the end of us / because without 2spot,
what would we be?

she sniffs up one line of powder

—you don't mind me doing this?

—no / yeah / well, yer know . . . whatever

—oh sorry / shit / I'm being stupid / sorry

—no / it's ok / actually . . .

—what?

—I will

—shit / you will / I mean / you will?

—why the fuck not?

—but . . .

—give it here

oh let's not think about this / let's just grab the

note out of her hand / stick it up the nostril, pinch shut the other / and then I'm sucking / sucking me that cloud of dust

—you ok?

—what?

—you ok?

—shit, yeah / oh yeah

—I don't know . . .

—ah no / it's fine / donna, it's fine / ok / ah . . .

ah yeah / it's got me hearing noises, whispers / a skullbuzz of static / and a tune that keeps circling / kinda fits in with the way that jody's shaking the floor from down below

—he played me some records, 2spot did / by his grandad

—what / danny? you know about danny?

—yeah, danny axle, that's it

—he played you that glamour album / good, isn't it?

—yeah / all that / all that music, yer know / like that . . .

—what / what is it?

—don't know

—what's that look about?

—what look?

—that look

—don't know, don't know / oh yeah / the music / about his family / 2spot's family / and the music, and all that / anyway, I said something to him

—ah / tricky subject

—I know, I know / he bit my head off

—he does the same to me

—he does?

—elliot / he's mad

—what / 2spot / what do yer mean?

—oh / not mad / just / well / there's something wrong with him, isn't there / I mean, I love him stupid and all that / the rhythm thing / but still . . .

—what is it?

she's looking at me / looking right at me / whispering . . .

—come on

and now, and now / she's standing up / how did she manage that?

—where to?

—bedroom

—oh / right / yeah

jesus . . .

forbidden songs

she's out of the room before I even know it /
and when I get to the foot of the stairs, it looks
like a million steps away, whatever's happening /
shit / that coke has done me in, on top of the
wine / too much / and with every step climbed, it
seems I focus more and more on myself, on what
I've done and how stupid I'm being / until, by the
top, I feel quite cold / almost in control / but then
I'm looking around the landing, thinking, which
bedroom did she mean / mine / or hers?

well / mine's still piled high with rubbish / a
little part of my mind saying, I'll have to get that
cleared, before I sleep tonight / and another little
part saying / wherever I sleep tonight . . .

donna's room / she's there, sitting on the bed
/ bathed in red light

—close the door, she says

—why are we whispering?

—you know, we shouldn't be doing this

—no

—because we're cheating on him

—right / erm . . .

—well sit down then

and then I'm beside her / donna's bed / 2spot's bed / their shared bed / and the cat's bed as well / bloody cat, following me everywhere / even to the edge of love / and donna says

—because I shouldn't be playing you this

—playing me?

and I see now / she's holding a record sleeve

—I got this from jody's room

she gives me the thing

—oh

—what's wrong?

—nothing / I thought . . .

oh stupid / so stupid

looking down / a garish cover / the photo floats an inch above the sleeve, and then falls into place / street scene, some ugly-looking teen punks / dressed like anorexic crows, with low-slung guitars / rabid scissor-shock of hair / the album's called *skull*, oh yeah, by the figs / on the back, four portraits, four names

mondo, fluxus, deezil, mule

—it's 1977, says donna

—I've heard of these / they played the last night of the circus / october 77

—that's right, says donna / I'm impressed / they never get mentioned

—near everybody was playing that night / the end of the line

—there's a buzzcocks bootleg, from the gig

—yeah

—jody sampled it / nicked a guitar line, for *scorched out*

—jesus / that's obscure

—oh yeah / that's jody for yer / you want to hear some?

—buzzcocks?

—the figs?

donna hands me a set of headphones

—what's this for?

—I can't listen to it, she says

—why not?

—against the law

—against the what?

—never mind / just listen

I look at the sleeve / the first song / *good times, bad times*

—are you ready? I'm turning it up

—what?

oh / shit / the noise / the shock-blast noise of it / right around the brain, captured there / blistering / bursting fire from ear to ear / and the vocals, screaming / speed fire / like a knife fire, scraping flesh / clean off the bone

good times, bad times! good times, bad times!

—christ!

even the good times turn out bad!

ripping the headphones off

—what's wrong? says donna, grinning / I thought you liked punk

—not this, not this

—what's it like?

—believe me / this is bad / bad punk

—only, you mustn't tell 2spot / that I let you hear it

—why not?

—it's his dad

—what?

it takes a while / everything slowed down, suddenly

until I'm looking at the sleeve again / the figs album / these four guys / mondo, fluxus, deezil, mule / all the players, slowed down / until every detail stands out

—which one is he? I ask

—I'm not sure

—fuck / what is it with 2spot / why's he so tight?

—he hates his father / really hates him

—why?

—you mustn't tell him I played this, you absolutely mustn't / he doesn't even know that jody's got the album / they're banned from the house

—donna, this is stupid

—I know, I know / it's just that / oh / something happened

—what happened?

—something nasty / he won't talk about it / he never talks

—tell me

there's a sound of movement from jody's room / she must've come up from the cellar / and before I can say a word, donna puts her finger to my lips, to keep me quiet / and all my body seems to be concentrated in that one spot, where her fingers touch my mouth / my eyes are drawn, to hers / magnetic to the moment

—he's in prison

—who is?

said around the finger / the touching finger

—the dad, 2spot's dad

—what for?

—I don't know

—donna . . .

—don't say anything

—donna? what's happening?

our eyes lock / so dark, with midnight-blue tears / I'm suddenly, intensely, aware of the colour of her skin / the difference we make, against each other / she takes her hand off my lips, touches her own with the wet fingers / jody is banging about next door, but I swear / we aren't making any noise, none at all

donna leans over, closer . . .

closer . . .

the love scene

and then I'm waking up, trying to anyway / I can't find the doorway, the exit sign / sometime and somewhere / it's the last night at the electric circus, I'm trapped there / with this band called the figs playing in my head, real loud / but they're playing our song for some reason / *scorched out for love* / and playing so rotten, so loud and so badly this black presence has entered my sleep, pressing a shadow onto me, strangling / the music, the music / I'm caught in the middle of pushing the song away, caught for ever, when I manage to climb upwards somehow / swimming upwards, through the shadows and the fur of the music

the *fur* of the music?

gallagher the cat is sitting on my chest / that single eye staring mad / the whole black moon of his enveloping pupil

I'm in my own bed, my own room / all the rubbish lies around, just dumped to one side / it's dark, with a pale, translucent shine from the window / a diseased streetlamp / I grope for my watch / ah, it's on my wrist, still / green figures bleeding at the edges / I pull the thing close, closer still

3.17

oh / get the fuck off me, mangy fucker!

what happened?

everything's quiet in the house, except for a strange, distant, unearthly noise / takes me a while to realise it's coming from inside my head / the dull fuzz of wine and drugs, a paste clinging to the skull / shit / I took some coke tonight / why the fuck did I do that / why the fuck?

that mustn't happen again / that mustn't

that mustn't happen again / that mustn't

and now / I'm lying on top of the sheets, fully clothed / trouble is, I can't remember when I came to bed, fell into bed / fell onto the bed / something like that

that mustn't happen again / that mustn't

and then I get this sudden, urgent desire to piss

the bathroom's along the corridor, past 2spot and donna's room / and then past jody's / no noise from either of them / once in the place, and when I turn on the light / screeching, the room lurches white-hot into me / jesus, like I've sucked the porcelain into my eyes / dirty, scummed up / a fat black spider darts like a blindness / and I take off in the opposite direction, hitting the wall / a picture falls to the floor, exploding

fuck / christ, that was loud / ok, ok / I'm keeping still, collecting the air in my lungs / waiting, waiting / and then finally, breathing

no noise / only the spider's tiny legs sliding on the porcelain, and the sound of my head, swimming through itself / so I do the business, and it takes an age and it makes a terrifying sound / but all the time I'm completely and utterly focused on a small, pink stain on the wall in front of me / remnants of the dream, still revolving / and I'm being watched, of course / gallagher's sitting on the bare floorboards, gazing intently at my willy and the piss that flows from it, never-ending

on the way back, I put my ear against donna's door / I'm sure I can hear something now, quiet noises from within / music, the saddest music / I'm trying to remember what happened between us, earlier on / was it good, was it bad / was it nothing whatsoever / was I even there when it happened?

something happened / nothing happened

I knock gently on the bedroom door

there's no answer / the noises continue / I knock again, slightly louder, and now surely that's a woman's voice, calling / softly, invitingly

under gallagher's baleful eye I open the door

oh

2spot's back / he's come back / I didn't hear him come back

the scene arouses itself from the darkness, takes shape / 2spot's lying on his back, wearing a tee-shirt / it's the least I've ever seen him wearing / donna's leaning over him, administering a caress / gently murmuring / and I shouldn't be here / I really should just walk away / slowly, quietly, forgetting with every step / yeah, do that

but 2spot's body is different from how I expected / somewhat leaner, more stretched / and I'm drawn to the sight, as though to a film, a slow-moving dirty video / it's the city's filtered moonlight that dirties them, not the act itself, which seems muted, almost surreal / translating 2spot's blond hair into a gleam of blackness

ah

it's not 2spot

he didn't come back

it's jody

I see it now / a flattened landscape ridged only with bone / a shadowed hermaphrodite, prone to receive / so peaceful in the waiting, she looks to be asleep / donna hovers tenderly, to give the love needed / and I notice almost accidentally that donna, like myself, is still fully clothed / she turns now, slowly around, her head moving as though

through clouded air / I'm not even sure if she
knows I'm here, not really / a shadow in the room

    gallagher pads silently towards the bed / and
leaps

    uh

    it's not love

    it's not love that's being given

    unless a syringe be love

    and pulsed flesh

    donna pushes the message home, into jody's
arm / so gently I can hardly believe that anything
will be squeezed out / and then I feel a swirling, as
though inside my own sweet, dissolving veins

    h

    the magic letter

    the needle digs deep, makes feed / and
something gets tempered

    donna looks at me once again, this time seeing
me for sure / and for the second time that night
she puts a finger to her lips

    as though to keep me quiet

    or else replace a kiss

Bass Instruction Manual

To wake the strings so tightly bound, let slide
The finger's nub along the neck from fret
To fret; from bridge to nut, the tones collide
And sound the joyous air! And yet, and yet . . .

If root of base desire the song deny,
In tempting play of lover's serenade;
No matter then how crafted skill apply:
Inside the heart remains a note mislaid.

plug me in, one time

did yer ever get danced / get skinned / did yer?

did you get some dance inside / all the way inside

and did yer blood start moving with it / singing with it / did yer sweat some?

I did / I got some, got me some / got me some dance, oh serious

loaded up on floor-thrill

like a bootleg rhythm-kill

and did yer ever get so danced, like yer couldn't feel any more / like where you ended, and the floor began / and the crowd / did yer get some crowd / did yer get some serious bootleg-type crowd right up inside your skull?

I did / got me some crowd like I couldn't feel any more

where the ending of the skin began

and where the crowd dissolved

drench and squeeze

and dissolve, into each other / the one great beast of love that dancers make / when the music grabs their hearts, spins them around, makes something new of them / even with the cheap-core slabs of noise, pounding from the speakers / no mercy / some deep-down concrete kiss of rhythm, to get the arse in gear

techzak / operation obliterate, down the club zuum

saturday night packed / enough to get the walls sweating / some kinda tingle skin-crawl / the noise and the lights and the lager and the shots and the too many lung-drags on cheapo ciggies / all doing the business / also, I'm still suffering from last night's mishap / and I really do need another drink / right now / oh yeah, but where's the bar, who moved the bar / and how come all nightclubs dissolve like this, around about this time of an evening / like I need a beacon-guide or a map or something.

radar sonics / jody's on the decks / dj fever /

and I know she hates playing this fleshcore stuff, except for the money it pulls / and what the fuck / nasty plastic beat mechanics / I let them drag me along / right out, onto the floor

dancers dancing, dance around me / and dancing around me, dancers dance

but wet through already, you know, and going under / swirl of hot / skulldrill in four time / I can't get the rhythm / don't even want to, but the club's banging down hard / oh yeah / jody's really shaking up the floor / transmitting black song up the ankles, thighs, dick, stomach and lungs / to the neck, the mouth, the networks of the head / where the tune gathers, explodes, becomes pure thought / floats free, top of the skull / gets caught in the lights, becomes a swarm of noise / starts to hammer back down

when someone pushes against me / falls against me

some dancer thrown by the music / all twisted sweated doubt like he can't believe what's happening to him / and then gone / caught by new rhythms / ok, jody's on the mix, working the transition so good between the heavy, heavy pounding

and this creeping new arrival

two records, playing at the same time, each fighting for breath / chaos twisters / tendrils of beat reach out, discordant, grab the sound, transform it / pulling apart, dragging bits of each tune between them

the dancers lose step momentarily, filling the rhythm void with shouts and cries / arms rising upwards, fingers stretching to pierce the laser beams, to grab at smoke / as the records gel, become one, you can actually hear the first tune being eaten alive by the second / great clusters of sound enveloping, and the crowd loves every moment / a massive cheer goes up / new beat / acceptance / let's dance!

but the new tune won't keep still enough for them / just flecks of noise, here and there / a wild scattering / no glue / but clouds and clouds and clouds and clouds and clouds / and twisting / turning / twisting turning away, away, away

jody's voice / chanting over the system, goading the crowd / telling them about the new sound / the glam damage sound / crying out

—bring it on, come on / bring on the damage / glam it up / come on / glam it up high!

it's the song / the liquid song / the glam damage song / our song / our fuckin' song / scorched out on the floor / and we're losing it / losing the crowd / because where's the beat / where's the stickiness / hands fall, arms drop down, whistles grow blunt / dancers move in slow circles, searching / some of them are leaving the crush / making space around me what the fuck is jody doing / like, where's the fuel?

until / suddenly / I hear myself come in / from nowhere, the bass painted so loud, so deep / it smothers the room / BOOM! one more time, come on / sonic BOOM! the floor cries with the feeling / blood pulse in fluid time / now 2spot, drum-distorted, enters the mix / like a panic attack, a mad battery, electric pulses / cracking the air, wide wide open / and it gets them somehow, just a few of them / just a few brave, foolish dancers who dare to find something within all this noise / because it has a beat all its own, and a subterfuge / the hidden rhythm / beneath, beneath, beneath the beneath / where the lone dancers dance, finding each other in the crowd's hard stare / passing virus / it becomes a show, an exhibition, a parade of strange

something that only a few can do / therefore, a code

a rough circle forms / sad laughing strangers, who can only watch the process / this sudden popping of the limbs any which way / this surprise collapsing of the hips and knees, jellified / and the slow pattern of the feet, like a wash of mathematics on the dancefloor / flow diagrams, moving not to the beats but the frequencies / jody's chanting again, the words through a lowdown pitchfilter

—scorched out for love / coming home to yer /
I said coming home to yer / damage style!

I count the dancers / six, seven / now eight,
nine / and while waiting for the tenth, across the
circle I see donna's face staring at me / staring
straight at me, that flash of symmetry, the never-
ending smile / all the way across the nightclub /
light bulb to light bulb, filter to filter / speaker to
speaker / and heart to heart / and right on cue,
jody brings the singing in

waiting for the world to learn
the contours of your skin

it's so tender / that somehow the dj's fingers
have brought the words back to the original / or
else the liquid flows around to meet itself / and not
just the sound, but the fact that donna, the singer,
is here to catch the song / just the fact that she's
here, listening / and that I'm here, watching / and
so tender, that jody's up in the box, playing this
song of mad love

that's the way of the world my friend
when a world comes to an end

and then 2spot is here as well / back from
wherever / putting his arms around donna / the
loving arms / curling round, to find out the secret
rhythms / the skin's rhythms / and I wonder how
much / I wonder how much he knows, really /

about   donna / about   jody / about   himself / and
what they all get up to in the dark

> *we throw it all away*
> *to start again*

as another person gets the beat / and another,
and another / filling up the floor with a love that's
never pure

ah shit, when all the broken children learn to
dance

check the technique

and now / and now with jody in the booth, working the groove / down below the people move / I'm standing beside her, watching the skill / her two hands, in circles of magic skim over the turntables / crossfading between them, working the records / two different vinyl mixes of *scorched out*

strictly private edition / direct from the globe / white label dreams

dragging beats from the deep / at the same time, a random globemix of the song is playing from the wave playback equipment / newly installed this stuff, and the crowd down below just don't know what's happening / three mixes, two stilled, the other fluid / and jody playing havoc with the patterns between them / now turning down the booth system / quiet enough to speak over

—you see now / we get them on vinyl / mix them around / add in the globe / juicy, eh?

kids are banging on the booth door,

demanding to know what the sound is / jody ignores the calls, all of them

—make them wonder, elliot / make them fuckin' wonder

oh yeah / the secret currents

I step towards the glass, gazing down into the club pit / swallowing the sight of it, the flood down there, the one huge flood of dance / magnetic attractions / because the liquid can't stop flowing / the music won't stop being played / the dj can't stop the mixing / and the people can't do nothing but move their butts around

—now watch this, says jody

she takes a second globe from the dj box / shakes it up, good and proper / now a knife appears / a thin blade / she's twisting the blade into the globe, the top of it, where the sealed valve is / what's she playing at?

move closer / move closer to find out

she's opened it somehow / jesus / some trick of the dj's wrist / squeezing something / oh yeah, a plastic eye-dropper / filling it with the stuff / a small vial / and then / and then / and then / oh listen, and then

she squeezes the drops of liquid onto one of the records / and more drops, onto the other / and then does the expert scratching thing / the needle sliding through the grooves so smoothly now

makes the music slip away and slither /
become a river

of fuck / jody turns up the monitors, right off
the scale / and it's like the whole club is moving
through space, taking off, going into orbit

just floating away

45 rpm / bpm infinity

more demands from the booth door

—what the fuck is that / what the fuck is that?

I look down once more, through the glass,
down to the floor / where all the people now
crowd, lost to the melting / even donna, donna
and 2spot / down there, lost together

in the melting of the plastic

zoom fever

the whole place caught tight and released, in
the wave of knowledge passing from the dj's
fingers / lost and found, to the dancers' hearts /
and the only thing I can't quite trace

is where the hell do I fit into the mix?

scorched out, club zuum remix

broken crazy dance noise of the samples
down in the stretch-out with bass overloading
the black vinyl splice of liquid tactics
lost
in the hidden BOOM knowledge chant
loop-dancer dripping a deep lament
of mad magic scatter honey
found
exploding bootleg skin splinters
nerve poison scraped from the shimmer
working a pop drag screech from the heart
lost
and taking a hit from blade strings
injection's dance fires up the groove glide
along the decks of tripwire
found
in the snare-time rain of cymbals drumfalling
through scratches of rhythm stolen and kissed
kaleidofunk dissolving
lost
in the tangle and crackle

beneath the buttons

somewhere later / I find donna lost in the dance / all on her own, out on the edge of the floor, making a trapped pattern / all her body, caught in motion / the drink in her hand, spilling

—donna?

—uh

—donna, come here

—what?

her eyes / fixed on some wingbeat, invisible / some place in the song, where the feelings float away easy / *scorched out* for ever / new versions, new rhythms to catch the crowd with / the floor's packed / I have to shout in donna's ear, full blast

—donna, what's wrong with you?

—nothing

—what happened last night?

—last night?

—did you take some, with jody / did you?

—I love you

—what?

—I love you, elliot / I fuckin' love you, I do

ok / she's out of it / well out

—and I love you too, donna

the beer spills down her dress

—here

she's holding the glass out towards me

—take it

shit

I take the glass / swallow the beer in one / and then donna's holding me by the arm / quite softly

—what's wrong? I ask

—it's 2spot

—what about 2spot?

she looks away from me / out into the crowd / right to where the dancing finds its centre / its mass / and I follow her eyes, all the way through / and then push through myself, forcing a way

they're not dancing

they're just watching

watching around some lonely lone dancer, dancing alone / caught in his own space

2spot

immaculately in time / with all the liquid groove that jody pours down

and I can't believe what I'm seeing / 2spot, with his jacket off / jacket off, and shirt off / his sweat-covered chest, stomach and arms, all on view / and criss-crossing all the flesh . . .

marks of the knife

cuts   and   splices / grooves   and   slices /
scabbed   and   fresh / opened / and   closed / and
reopened / in a map of pain / all scratched out / in
blood recorded / remixed
and then
broken

underground jam

and now, and now, and now / beneath the dancing / the studio clock, at one glance it tells me two o'clock / five minutes later, ten past midnight / I can't remember how I got this stretched out / full-length on the floor, a cushion against the wall to support my shoulders / with this head full of singing, like I've swallowed a voice, a stranger's voice / 2spot's moving around the instruments, the drumkit and the decks, searching for something / he's making a strange chirping sound

—what yer lost? I ask him

nobody hears me / nobody's paying any attention to me / jody's putting on a record, just for us / *scorched out*, one more version / liquid ambient style / donna's chattering away to her-self, so happy with the way the song went down tonight / wasn't she all upset, only a while ago / was that tonight, I wonder / seems like another planet / and 2spot / still doing the strange noise routine / fully clothed, wasn't he naked earlier / and covered with stars / stars?

scars, I mean / covered with scars

when was that?

I raise a hand to my face / damp with sweat, and barely there beneath the fingers

look at the clock / quarter past three already / somebody should get that thing fixed

2spot is still making that funny noise and looking behind the amplifier cabs / now he's rubbing his fingers together, like some kind of secret rhythm

—you want some of this? asks jody

I look over / the dj's pouring out the drinks / she's really messing with the preparation / doing what? and with what? and what's that in her hand?

—we can't start unless we're all here, says 2spot

and I'm wondering just what it is we can't start, and who else needs to be here to start it / but then the drinks get handed around / bourbon / and the first sip, the burn so sweet, so scorching

so scorched out, all the way down

gets another tune going / counterpoint to the one already lodged within me

so I lie back and let the music happen / we are the glam damage, I think to myself / we are the damagers of glamour and here we live our lives, like glamorous damage

from the way my head is angled, I can see

behind one of the amps / right into the shadows where the music lives / and I fix on that point, right there where the shadow starts to move / where the music starts to move in the shadows, prowling out from the amp like a cat / and then it is a cat, a black and sooty cat

—gallagher!

—at last, there you are, says 2spot

—what's the cat doing here? I ask

—he came with us, says donna

—did he?

2spot is letting the cat lick at the drink in his glass

—what's he doing to that cat?

—feeding it, says jody

—leave that cat alone

—ah, the guy's floating, says 2spot

is he talking about me?

—I thought he could take his drink

is he talking to me, or the cat?

—I can drink you under the / under the / under the . . .

—go on then, he says / drink yer drink

so yeah, whatever

—you like that? says the cat

—oh yeah / got a kick

and then 2spot's laughing at me / and donna, laughing also / and the cat, laughing / and even jody laughing / who's never been seen to laugh

before, so I really must've taken one too many
one too many

I really must / somehow / get myself / on / my /
feet

—you want some more? says jody

I roll over / 2spot's pouring more whisky into
my glass / and jody's kneeling beside him, holding
something over the drink

a tube of glass, it looks like / bulbous and soft
at one end / sharpened / sharpened down to a
blue vanishing

squeeze

jody makes a slow squeeze of the bulb

ah / it's a . . .

and a tiny blue droplet appears / on the
vanishing

and drops / slowly

slowly

splosh

into my drink

ah

what's this?

—go on then, says donna, coming close / drink
yer drink

—give him more, says 2spot

and squeeze

I see now / the eye-dropper in her hand / and
I'm trying to remember where I saw such a thing
/ why, not that long ago . . .

slowly, slowly / squeezing the sky / burning
blue

for some reason my eyes / won't let go of the
sparkle of it

falling now

and

splosh

into my drink

—more for everyone, says 2spot

and then jody's going around, doing the
routine into all the glasses

and it comes to me then

oh shit / they're putting the music / the tune /
the wave / into my drink, into all the drinks / now
drinking / now all of them / jody, 2spot and donna
/ drinking the drinks / turning to look at me

—what's wrong? asks 2spot / don't you like it?

—he loves it, says donna

—he fuckin' loves it, says jody

—fuckin' well loves it rotten, says the cat

until all the voices mingle

mingle / falling / tingle / singing

like a song in my

like a song

like a

bass addiction

alone / alone / alone now / studio bed / waking from / waking up from / coming to / coming round from / with no knowledge of / no knowledge / having moved, from the floor / the room is empty / only the cat to tell me I'm still the same person, in the same place / at the same time

the clock / it reads half past one / which can't be right, can it / it must be later than that / because *scorched out* is still playing / and nothing lasts for ever

not even music

I don't know where donna, jody and 2spot have got to / and to be honest I don't care / only one thing matters / adding some noise to all the noise that was ever made

to stop the tune from ever ending / ever ending

the fender's at home, but the studio's got a house model / nothing fancy, just four strings and a body and an amp to plug it into / the world / and I play / along with the track, new lines / spirals and showers / pulses and kicks / and all the flames and the licks of the wrist / no tricks, not slick / just the flick of a switch and a hit from the tips of the fingers / a riff that lingers / over samples and singers / and the twin-deck ninjas

and 2spot's drumming, as my becoming

ah listen / it's the best I ever played, all my life

and it gets me thinking about how my playing has just got better and better, since joining the damage / putting it down to a good band at last, and a girl to impress

but now

recalling all the drinks I've been downing, and what the hell was being put in them

oh fuck

they really took me, didn't they?

they really fucking took me

making strange

I find the band upstairs in the little kitchen / all gathered around the electric stove

—here, stupid, says donna / turn it up

—yeah, says 2spot / more heat, more heat

—I'm doing it, says jody / I'm doing it

push through

there's a pan on the stove, quite small / a circle of cooking foil crimped over the top of it / aluminium soft / the foil bulges / pulses / as though something is trapped inside

—what the fuck?

on the work surface beside the stove / four globes / all empty / all with the seals broken

—ah, the bassman, says 2spot

—how yer feeling? says donna

—fucked over

—yeah / well . . .

—well nothing / what the hell / since when, since when / doping my drinks, all the time / since when / since the first rehearsal / the juice / you can't do that to a person / you can't do that!

donna shrugs

—got yer funky

—jesus!

—and that's just by drinking it

I'm almost / almost, almost

—elliot, says 2spot / you gonna hit her, you'll have to hit all of us

—we all did it, says jody / you up for that?

—ah!

I hit out at the first thing / the first innocent thing / gallagher / just send that cat flying

shrieks and hisses / and then silence in the room / donna, jody and 2spot, all looking at me / these three faces / I've known them, what / five, six weeks / not long, and not much / but jesus, I have some love for them / I do, believe me

—do they know about this?

I'm pointing at the contraption on the stove

—who?

—the makers?

it just gets them laughing, and why not

—fine, you're all mad

—come on, says 2spot / who's first?

—me, me! says donna

—donna . . .

—elliot, let me do this

I can hardly think straight about what's going on / just watching from the sidelines as 2spot sticks a drinking straw through the foil / blue smoke rises up it, reaching the end where his thumb traps the outlet

the singer bends down / and one more time I say

—donna, please / you don't know what it'll do

and then 2spot removes his thumb, letting donna get her lips in there, clamped around the straw / the smoke swirls up the tube, into her mouth / immediately she pulls back

—don't cough, says 2spot / just don't start coughing

he's got his finger over the straw again, watching all the time as donna takes the stuff down into her lungs

finally

—ah

she breathes out / through the nostrils / clouded

—shit / that's hot

and then we're all just looking at her / waiting until she smiles

—well / I'm alive

—what's it like? asks jody

—nothing yet / a bit dizzy

—jody? says 2spot / your turn

and have you noticed / how 2spot's in charge tonight / this music thing, it's changing him / the cold passion, the crazy control / all the things we love his drumming for, now made real / and the smoke he holds in his hands / in his hands / in his beautiful playful hands

jody comes forward / takes her hit / no trouble

—there you go, says 2spot / easy does it

then he turns to me

—bassman?

I shake my head / no

—you shouldn't have done it, I say

—what, make you brilliant?

—you should've said

—and have you refuse?

donna wanders past me, out the door / her eyes already far away

—oh yeah, says jody / let's make some music / come on you two

and she follows donna / leaving 2spot and me, in the tiny kitchen

—I might not have refused, I say to him

—yeah, there's that / come on, sit down

2spot searches in a drawer one-handed / finds a wooden clothes peg / with this he crimps the straw shut / then he sits at the dirty table, and I slide in opposite

—you know, he says / I absolutely loved tonight / didn't you?

—it's good

—all them people / dancing like that

—2spot, it's the liquid

—I know

—it's the liquid doing the work, making us good

—so?

—it's . . .

—it's what? cheating? oh come on, bassman / it's what you put in / it's different now / bands won't be the same, once this takes off / it's not about finished product any more / it's the process / making the process happen, that's all we're doing

—but smoking it?

—might not do anything

—drinking it . . .

—drinking it makes you play the bass like you never did / so then? smoking turns you into the best player of all time / just on the off chance, what do you say?

again, I shake my head

2spot looks around, and then turns cold / he gets a grip on my arm, a drummer's grip / down hard

—do you believe, he asks / that every human being has the right to damage themselves?

—jesus, what a question

—you spent some years doing it

—yeah, but / and get off my arm

—well, do you? do you believe in the right?

—you know the answer, 2spot

—of course I do / as long as no one else is damaged along with them

—aye, that's the excuse / but damage reaches out, into the world / it reaches out anyway / family, friends . . .

—your wife?

—donna told you?

—she tells me everything

—does she?

—I know you like her

—do you?

—and you know I've had trouble / in the life?

—some / donna wouldn't say

—she doesn't know / not really

—you don't treat her right, 2spot / yer just don't

—nobody knows / nobody

finally, he takes his fingers off me

—elliot / this is all that matters to me

—what / drugs?

—the music, the music / it's the only thing I've got

I see all the pain in his eyes, trapped there

—2spot . . .

—the only thing

—what is it / what's happened?

—the music, the music . . .

he's shaking his head / gently, side to side / some frozen rhythm he can't escape / his eyes, wet / and his shirt / open at the neck, so unusual /

and just about seen there / the scars / what makes that / what makes somebody do that to themselves?

ah / if I could only reach out to him / touch him

—the music . . .

but nobody can

I look over at the stove / the thin plastic straw / the smoke inside it, gathered ready / stand up, go over / unclamp the peg / the smoke starts to escape

I let it drift for a second or two

and then stop the end of the straw with my thumb

—2spot . . .

—uh

—come on then

slowly, he stands up / turns to face me

—just the once, mind

—oh aye, just the once

he comes to the stove / and the strangest thing / he holds my hand / he holds my hand as he bends to the straw / I let go the smoke, and he sucks

and then / quickly now / I do the same

hot / the bitter taste / and yet sweet / like all the dreams I've been having lately

and out / release / engaged to the sun / one time, two time / hands still holding / and 2spot's face, turned on

—what now? I say

—we go and play, what else

so, down the stairs to the studio / gentle and slow / I can't feel anything, beyond the very slow and gentle world we all live in / down to where the dj and the singer are lying on the bed together / gallagher curled up between them

—ah, we didn't give the cat any, says the drummer

—the cat's had enough, says the bass player

the drummer sits down on the floor near the bed / drums forgotten / and the bass player sees the bass standing against the wall / and he leaves it there / because now he's on the floor as well / with music playing / somewhere, a globe spinning / spinning, as the bass player crawls over to the bed, to join the singer, the dj and drummer there / a taste of flowers, petrol, as the bass player's face presses against the drummer's hair / and the cat, purring like crazy

all the air that gathers, seems blue like the smoke / like the smoke in the lungs, in the veins / and blue / like the music

only the cat seems deeply black / the bass player reaches out / to stroke the fur

the world is a blue sunrise and he can't think why, especially when his hand goes right through the cat's fur / like smoke

right through the cat's skin

right through into the cat
the burning hot-flesh insides of the cat
and the bass player follows his hand all the
way through

smoked out for love, punk filter dissolve

all the way through
              lost in the drumfall
        dripping caught and twisted splinters
      scratching tactics   mad magic
                      rhythm skin explosion
          kaleidosonic scatter of bass fire
              turntable BOOM honey funk
      deep in the bootleg

taking a drag from the loop dancer vinyl
                amplifying samples
      down along the decks of tripwire heart glide
          smoking the grooves
        scraped from the shimmer of BOOM song
                  waiting for the world to
          bruise crackle pop dissolve

              the noise the noise

kaleidopunks

oh / shit / the noise / the shock-blast noise of it
/ right around the skull, captured there / blistering
/ bursting fire from ear to ear / and the vocals,
screaming / speed fire / like a knife fire, scraping
flesh / clean off the bone

shit / what is this song?

of burst guitar / hammer clang / breaking,
falling / all the cries of madness / so bitter /
choked, spat rapid, crippled, thrown aside

good times, bad times!
good times, bad times!

oh yeah, that's the one / so now I'm pushing,
through the crowd / to the edge of a creaking
balcony / looking down on a four-piece band, like
a blow of raging / and a singer who spits out
garble / spike of the tongue, plunging, blurred to
the brain

even the good times turn out bad!
even the good times turn out bad!

rhythm cut / pulled along / feeling the music skip like a vinyl jag / like someone spins my clock around / all around the turntable, just a few seconds / blackness, folding / and then jerked apart

oh yeah / hi there / the name's elliot / elliot hill

down / down tight / and tighter now / down on the floor / caught in the pack, the jumping flesh machine, with the jagged spikes / and there on the stage, glimpsed at the top of every leap / it's the figs / the fuckin' crappy figs band / and I can't stop moving, despite how crap it all is / ah yeah, now I'm a dancer / a gunshot dancer / a crazy tight-spot jumper / king of the pogo / I'm a bonecore junkie reverber / hit by the bass / the snare, the skin and wire / the sonic boom bullets / oh please, come on / screaming out / the cheap and nasty three times / cheap and nasty three times / say it loud now / cheap and nasty three times

good times, bad times!
bad, bad, bad!

as the music starts to really lose it / as the people start to jeer, and the bass player just takes off / just throws himself from the stage, into the crowd / sailing

and then I'm smoke / liquid smoke, caught in the edit

and sucked away / dissolving / and down / along / down and along / catching sparks, in the grooves of the night / band after band after band / moments of the fall / warsaw / cooper clarke / the drones / the worst / the negatives / the prefects / many more / seen in glimpses / and the fans / place them up there with the players / the wall to wall mess of people, gathered / night of the closedown

upon this day / october 2, 1977

the electric circus club / a final parade / of the loud, the fast, the dirty and the strange

landing cold, back on the balcony, clinging / and now, it's the magazine band down there / suddenly, out of nowhere / and who the fuck is this kid, he can fly like that / through the grooves?

oh yeah / hi there / the name's elliot / elliot hill

they call me kid bruise, with the pins in the heart, and the clothes that cling with sweat and metal / kid crackle, with the hair that climbs the rafters / goaded by sweat and wax and talcum powder / as the place uncurls around the strangeness / gets a new dress to wear / all torn and tattered, and yet studded with safety pin pearls

look down

see the people breathing the wave / dancing,

as one / tasting the battery's kiss / and one of them, a drifting girl, torn from the pack

I know that girl / I know that girl / her name, what's her name now?

jody . . .

ah / she made it as well

and then smoke / ghosting around me / the body pulled open / away / into a cut jump / like somebody dragged a stylus right across

and down / further along the balcony

watching the buzzcocks / the powder fuse / pumping sizzle through the veins electric / with the singer's voice, a plastic charm of camp and dark / careless passion, so fast and lazy / ecstatic chaos shakers / a scratch of spiral, enfolding

oh yeah / it's here now, the feeling / captured / all the fog grabbed and gathered, into the skull / the heart, beating up love / unpinned, at last / and these clothes I'm buckled and dressed and skin-pressed in, and crowd-caressed in / made sticky by the rhythm that grabs me / oh yeah / like the strings of the cheapest guitars

—I was born to be / I was born to be here

something . . .

something like that anyway

as the girl beside me says

—come on, we have to find him

squeezing around to meet the stranger / and knowing already, from somewhere strange,

her name is donna / donna, donna, donna / a
stranger, come to whisper

—elliot, come on!

—what?

—we have to find 2spot

—who?

—2spot, 2spot!

—oh yeah, find 2spot / who?

—his dad / he's after his dad!

she's pulling on my arm / out of the crowd-
push

—what's happening?

—I don't know, I don't know / come on

and pulled

and cut / like a blade of mist / scissored

landed / floor of the gig, caught in the surge /
pogo my flesh alive now / and the bones and
muscle, powered by riffs and kisses / lost riffs
and lost kisses / the music / powered by the rain,
saliva, giros, bruises, crackles of feedback, chord
patterns, bad love and the flowers of pop, dug
from the bargain basement of the heart / and I'm
thinking

—I was born to be here

to hear the music some more, and more
deeply / and then to think

—no / not born to be here / I was born here /
that's it / born here, right at this gig / these
moments / with the girl called jody / right there

beside me, catching the rhythm / set loose / and set aflame

—we did it, elliot / we fuckin' did it!

fingers pass through each other's grasp / and then slide away / along the music in slices / with the singer's words, chanted out now

—time's up

the last ever song / and then

twisting / I'm gone

shit

I can't get fixed / I can't get a fix on it

away / out on the edge of the noise / where somebody pushes against me / one face into another / with mists of lavender, caressing the air / and a smell of petrol, as though the night were about to catch fire / something touched upon, long ago / half remembered / tingling

—2spot!

—get out of the way

he throws me away / right into the girl / the other girl / yeah, donna / that's her name / I'm catching it now

—elliot, stop him!

and this time I can actually hear the song speeding up / buzzed and blurred / sucked from the grooves / spinning

down / down hard this time

outside

a genuine punk love song, maybe maybe

outside / feeling now the sudden cold frizzle of air / a bunch of punks hang around the doorway / one of them spray-painting the slogan TIME'S UP on the wall / with the song still playing from inside / a biscuit-tin rattle, as befits the night / the frozen punk moon / the punk clouds that mask the high-rise flats opposite / the bottle that falls from there

to smash beside a young punk couple / the two of them, wrapped together / all pins and studs, locking / punk kissing / the guy looks at me and says

—what you staring at?

—I'm not . . .

—well fuck off, ok

—dave / come on, let's do it

—yeah, sue / oh yeah

break-off / and hand in hand, they're walking away around the corner of the building / towards the back, where the punk cars are parked / and as I follow behind, I can't help feeling I'm trapped in some kind of story here / a punk fairy tale / one that only I know the ending of

their car, parked on the far side of the ground / some kids are guarding it / the guy pays them something, tells them to clear off / the kids go running past me

—fuckin' bastard punk rocker, one of them shouts

and then gone

dave and sue

those names . . .

dave is opening the back door of the car, not the driver's door / what's going on / and now / and now they're both climbing inside, into the back / the door shuts after them / the punk moon caught in the windows, right there

right there where

jesus / what's the urge I have, to just walk over there and watch?

something brushes against my feet / I look down, it's a cat / a filthy black punk cat / I kick it away, and for the first time that night I feel in charge of myself / I mean, just look at these clothes I'm wearing / the white baseball boots / the tight black jeans / the leather jacket, just a few pins here and there / some badges / a ripped-open tee-shirt

and this is my night, I just know it is

so / I set off, slowly, towards the car / the

creaking, cold punk car / they're doing it in there,
aren't they / doing the dirty / and where's the love
in all that / but yer know, maybe it is, to them /
maybe it's a punk love, to them / doing the mean
down and dirty

something squelches, under my foot / ah now
look / dogshit, all over the new baseball boot /
would you credit it / and what's that, something
glittering, stuck to the sole / like a diamond / but
look more closely / it's a 10-pence piece, right in
the smelly, sticky lump of it

mean down and dirty, but lovely / so lovely

at the car now / seeing the moon enraptured in
the dark of the glass / and when I put my eyes
against the

oh shit

what's happening to me?

not born to be here

not born here

but made here

I was fuckin' well made here!

I stumble back, away from the window / into
something / falling / it's that cat / that filthy cat,
getting in the way / the cat of smoke / the what?
the cat of what?

falling / smoked out for / smoked out for /
smoked out for . . .

and the cat brushes against me

—oh fuck

comedown city

—oh fuck . . .

—elliot . . .

—no / fuck / jesus!

—elliot, calm down

—what's wrong with him?

—hold him / hold him!

—fuck off!

I'm standing, barely standing now, like the world is a tilt-play dancefloor / and I can't tell who's pressing the buttons, who's speaking, and I don't really care, except that at last I'm back / the studio / down to earth, back in the land of the living / wherever, whatever

—it's ok / it's ok, I just need to / shit / fuck off will yer!

—elliot . . .

it's donna, talking to me / trying to hold me, touch me / console me

—you had a bad time?

—yeah / bad / it was . . .

I shake my head a couple of times, trying to rattle something loose

—2spot's still under

it's jody speaking now / and pointing over to where the drummer sleeps tight in a corner / we've all moved since we went under / moved apart / jody's trying to rouse 2spot out of his trip / I turn to donna

—jesus / that was some strange . . .

—I know

—you'll never guess what I just saw / christ, that's powerful stuff

—yeah / isn't it / where did you go?

—go? I went to the / yeah, fuck / the electric circus / oh / it was real / so real

—no / I mean, where did you go, when we went after 2spot?

—what?

—you left us there

—shit / what / you mean, you were there / you were fuckin' well *there*?

and it's all I can do to stop myself from running a million miles

—donna . . .

—we were there, elliot / it took us there!

her eyes / filled with wonder / desire / the pupils huge with gathered sight

—but / but how?

—I don't know / an hallucination

—but we all went there / jody . . .

the dj looks up

—we did it, elliot / we fuckin' did it!

and those words / the same words she said to me in the trip

I go over to her, looking down at 2spot / curled up tight, bedazzled, as though he's still down there, in there, out there, wherever, whenever / floating through the rhythms

—jody, says donna

—what?

—I don't think you should . . .

—what?

—jody, he's not going to like it / he was arguing in there / with his dad / I saw them

—what's wrong with you / come on, help me here

—jody, he's coming round / watch out

—what?

—arghhh!

it's like a feedback scream, dragged from one of the guitars we've just been inside / just 2spot's voice, coming up, scratching fire / and his eyes, clicking straight into burn-mode / and his arms, straight out to grab at jody's neck

—ugh!

—fucker!

—2spot!

donna and I move in / and it takes everything we've got, to break the grip / until, finally, 2spot lets go, and jody falls back / and then I'm on 2spot, just getting my arms around him somehow, pulling him close / and jody's crying, pleading . . .

—elliot, I swear / I swear, I never knew

—you fuckin' well did know / you sampled him / you sampled the bastard

—elliot, no / just the buzzcocks / the circus / and somehow

—and somehow you fucked with me / one too many times

—the rest got caught in it / in the samples / elliot / I don't know how

—let me up!

—you sure? I ask

—let me up

so, I let him go / it's a stretched-out moment, as he gets jody in his sights / and then he turns away, shaking his head

—it's not real, elliot, says donna / it's a trip, that's all / come on, eh / let's talk calmly now

but no / he's still shaking his head / putting his hands up to it now, all through the hair / the careful hair, all messed up / all sweaty / the grease on it, all sticky

—2spot . . .

donna's reaching out / out / out / daring to

—no!

all that rhythm, lost in a moment

—2spot!

—that's it, jody / that is it / I'm gone / do you hear / the job is done!

the last words

we can hear him clattering up the stairs / away from us / away / leaving us / a terrible silence, falling all around

broken finally, by donna

—jody . . .

jody's got nothing to say / nothing left to give / she's just sitting there, still on the floor / stroking the cat / she's stroking the fuckin' cat

—jody / do something, please

—do / do what?

—I don't know / I don't know

donna collapses / right into screaming

 —I don't fuckin' know!

limbo time

stranded, rhythmless / with no beats to our lives, just living them / living them like ghosts, moving through the days / the first day, and the second / and then the third, the fourth, the fifth / a week passes, slowly, so slowly

—he'll be back, I say to donna / he always comes back

but he doesn't / he can't / he won't

first single ready to be released / with a promotional tour set up by the zuum label / we were gonna play it out, live / with jody spinning the wheels, and donna singing, and me on the bass / and 2spot

and 2spot on the drums

and 2spot on the drums

ah shit

so, the counting of the seconds, the minutes, the days / the long hours of waiting / minus the living blue soul of the band, it's all just counting

two weeks, no 2spot / no music, no plug-in

and it's strange / because if 2spot hadn't

run off like this / I think it would've been me / running off / just getting away from there / all the madness / all the cheating they'd done on me

ah / what does it matter / they're just kids really, messing about

but this 2spot thing / I don't know, it's got me worried / and the way donna's taking it / not talking to anyone / staying in her room a lot / barely eating / losing the smile / well, I can't just take off easy / not yet, not yet / something's holding me

and I know she blames jody, that's another problem / for the use of the circus sample / but how was jody supposed to know / it's the fault of the liquid

the fault of the liquid

and what now / with the liquid

do we tell the makers / do we keep it secret / do we pour it all away, down the sink, down the toilet bowl / or do we carry on, as best we can / making the music

and the house / 2spot's house / all the equipment / the night he left, 2spot took the van, left everything else / what to do about all that / should we move out / move on / get new stuff / or just carry on, as best we can / making the music, the music

and then the zuum label release a choice version of *scorched out for love*, strictly vinyl / if this works out, they'll move in on the whole wave music production and playback system / one time I hear the song being played on the radio / just a late-night job, yer know / but so good to hear / and so bad / knowing what it represents

three weeks, no 2spot / no sign or sound / no clue

and we actually dare to start talking about the future / the possibilities / but where do you find a new drummer / one as good as 2spot?

you find them nowhere, nowhere at all

—he'll be back, I say to donna / he always comes back

but he doesn't / he can't / he won't

and then, one day / jody turns up with a drum machine

zuum records shelled out / a real state-of-the-art rhythm maker / the dj's in charge of the beats, of course / with me helping out here and there / learning the basics / because what's the alternative / only donna stays away from it / and I know that jody and I will have a job with her / getting her to sing again

ah shit

where the fuck is he?

one time / I catch jody alone in the kitchen, brewing up something / a little foil-covered pan of something sweet, and smoky / and I don't even talk to her / no shouting, no screaming / I just grab that pan off the stove / pour the whole lot, the smoking shit / right down the sink / and jody lets me, she just lets me do it

maybe she's doing this all the time now / forever journeying / becoming the rhythm

anything / to escape the minutes

the minutes, the hours, the days / all counted, away

all the waiting made so much worse, when *scorched out* goes into the charts at number 26 / and really, we should be singing, and laughing / and we do, jody and I, we try a little of that / but donna won't have it / she just won't admit what's happening

and then / weird thing / one morning I finally persuade donna to come out with me / just out of the house, yer know / the first time / shopping / whatever

and as we go through the door, suddenly, donna says

—2spot!

and there's the van / 2spot's van parked in the usual spot

donna running to it

but

no / it's just the van / empty

left in the night like an offering

lost boys, lost girls

—didn't it worry you?

—what?

—all those scars on his body / what was he doing, cutting himself?

—he never did

—well, somebody did

—no / I mean he never did it, not in front of me

we're sitting in the coffee bar of the library / and given what we're about to do, there's little point in hiding anything away / and donna's eyes tell the tale

—it killed me / every time / every time he came back from one of his trips / there would be new cuts / oh, maybe this is stupid, but

—but what?

—I think maybe if / yer know / if 2spot did what jody did / well then . . .

—heroin?

—well then / he wouldn't have to hurt himself

—he'd hurt himself

—yeah, but not in that way

—not in that way, no

her coffee's going cold / and she's stirring use-
less sugar into it

—is that what you do / with jody / stop her
hurting herself?

—me?

—that night / in the bedroom / I saw you

—did you?

—donna, you know I did

—that night / that night was just me and
jody . . .

—yeah?

—helping each other

—oh yeah? and what do you get out of it?

—love

—love?

—just love / just yer know, friendly love / with
2spot running off all the time / I mean, what am I
supposed to do?

—I see / and you're not taking yourself?

—elliot, don't you know me?

—I'm not sure / do I?

—you've got to understand / jody, 2spot and
me / all three of us / we're very close

—yeah, I get that

—we look after each other / and that's why . . .

—I know

—2spot doing this to me . . .

—yeah, I know

—he's never been away this long before /
what's he gonna come back like / can you tell me,
please / what's he gonna be like?

I can't answer / I just can't / and the way donna
looks at me then / letting me know, that all the
love she feels / will never slip away

—we can help him, can't we, elliot / when he
comes back this time / we can say, no more
secrets, 2spot / we can say that to him, can't we?

—yeah / we can / no more secrets

then we walk through into the reference library
/ starting the search / looking through micro-
fiches / databases / old copies of the music mags
/ local newspapers / plugging names into search
engines / turning them loose, dragging them back

until / finally / we find what we're looking for

in the pop music archives

late in the year of 1981, just after the release of their third album, a band called the figs split up / in payment for some unspecified remark, the vocalist with the band had physically attacked a member of the audience at one of their concerts / it was not the first such incident / the vocalist, commonly known by the name deezil, was sent to prison for a year

—that's him, says donna / deezil / that's 2spot's dad

in the autumn of 1995, with promises from the singer that he had changed his ways, the group embarked on a short tour of the north-west / it was called a comeback tour / but really, they were coming back from nowhere

the motivation for the reunion is difficult to imagine / it can't have been money / but just enough old punks still yearned for angrier, spikier days, to make it worth the while / also, there was a slight wave of nostalgia for more passionate times / the band decided to record two new songs as a single / they booked a day in a back-street recording studio / a twenty-four hour block booking, plenty of time for the two songs, and for anything else that might evolve from a pressurised jam

basic tracks were laid down, and then the group started to improvise, searching for ideas / nothing much came of these sessions / at 10.15 that night they decided to abandon the work, leaving the single in its original, rough-hewn form / they sent the engineer home, and retired to the nearest pub

just as last orders were being called, deezil announced that he had found an idea for a new vocal line / the other musicians wanted only to drink their beers, maybe go on to a club / deezil however was keen to carry on working / he would go back to the studio alone, and then meet them in the club later on / at the last moment, the bass player decided he would join the singer / the bass player was known as mule

the rest of the band left the club at 1.30am / having seen no sign of deezil or the bassist, they walked over to the studio / the recording light was on, and the tape machine rolling / however, no music could be heard through the monitors / they looked through the glass partition

at first, they report, they could see nothing at all / the studio looked quite empty / then they saw somebody lying on the floor / it was the prone figure of mule / next, they noticed the blood, splashed on the soundproofing / and then . . .

they see deezil / the singer is slumped against a wall, smiling / smiling . . .

the facts, such as they are / deezil's real name was george axle / he was thirty-eight years old / in a most vicious attack he had set about mule, using the bassist's own instrument as a weapon / mule suffered terrible injuries to the head and the hands / the hands, especially the hands . . .

the trial took place in early 96 / george axle pleaded not guilty to the crime / the jury listened in silence to the tapes of the incident, faithfully recorded in painful detail by the studio's equipment / the argument had started over a simple musical error the bass player had made / they heard deezil shouting his threats to cripple his fellow musician

—you'll never play again, you bastard / you'll never play again!

and then the thuds of the guitar, swung by the neck / against flesh, against bone / and the screams . . .

the threat proved true

the jury found the singer guilty / grievous bodily harm, with intent / taking into account the previous incidents of violence, and the particular viciousness of this latest attack, the judge locked george axle away for a period of six years

the reports stated simply that the singer had been under severe emotional pressure recently, following lengthy divorce proceedings / and a forced separation from his only child, william, a boy of thirteen

—oh, 2spot, says donna

—william / that's his name

—that's his name

two photographs of the criminal / one taken at the trial, his face set in fierce denial beneath the gelled-back hair / another from the sleeve of the third album / it was the same face / dirty blond hair crafted into spikes, and the same emotion on view / exact same / the eyes set tight in a punk glaze

—jesus, says donna

—I know, I know

—six years / he must be coming out soon

—most probably out already

—now we know why 2spot is so ashamed / of his father / oh, I wish I'd known this earlier

and then a comment in one of the papers about a troubled family, led us to another, even more disturbing report

that in 1977, george axle's father had killed himself / the well-respected musician, danny axle, found lying in a hotel bathtub, his wrists cut / he was forty years old

—shit

—no wonder, no wonder / 2spot loved his grandad, so much / oh god, elliot . . .

—yeah, I know / but look at the date

—what about it?

—donna, the date he killed himself / oct 3, 1977

—but . . .

—yeah / 2spot wasn't even alive then / and all those stories about how his grandad had taught him everything / given him the name and everything

—I don't understand / he made it all up?

—and not only that / the day danny axle died . . .

—what else?

—well, it's the day after, isn't it

—after? I don't understand / after what?

—the last night at the electric circus

beatbox display unit

later that same day / I go down into the cellar of the house to practise my bass-lines / jody's out for the night, and I don't mean down the pub / she's been on the screaming jitters all evening / donna was keeping her company, of course / on the blunt end of the needle / so it's quiet / peaceful / I'm alone with the walls and the damp and the cobwebs / sometimes, you practise alone, and the strings really hum / I've got the cellar lights out / graphic displays and LEDs alone to shine my flickering way

it's the first time I've played since 2spot ran off

and here I am now, doing ok / living with it / setting the echoes ringing in the dark / getting the buzz and soft rasp of the metal / fingers singing / I get all that down to the bone, and decide to play along to the new drum patterns

like I said, the drum machine, it's the latest model / loaded high with all the presets and whiz-bangs you could ask for / jody's an expert at the computers, so she's made us some digital madness, one for each song / all coded inside the box, press of a button / and I have some small fun messing about with the beats, playing new bass-lines / changing the old ones so they play against the metronome / trying to get some half-ounce of the old glam damage back in the music

now the machine, it's got a built-in sampler / just a sweet little unit hung on the side / as many switches as you could hope for, but simple enough to figure / sound grabber / a wire and a jack, and a direction of flow / I make a direct feed from our tape machine to the sampler, and then select one of 2spot's old practice tapes / choosing a broken-down moment of bliss, I send it travelling down the line / into the beatbox, stretched out and magnified

ah yeah, let the thing play / caught in the loop

then take up the bass, making with the beat fever / rattling the deep-down / in the dark, and getting darker / and loud, and getting louder / late, and getting later / hard, sweet and juicy / harder, sweeter, juicier / I guess I'm just trying to play the feelings off me / make it clean / and maybe / well, yeah / it's a little bit like 2spot's playing along with me / oh yeah, just a little

oh man, I make some noise / make me a stew / rich and thick and slow and hazy and as loud as fuck and I don't care who knows it / I make the house near shake the dark down, with vibrations all through the walls / and so totally lost in the sound, there's no way I can tell how long she's been standing there by the door / stops me dead

—I thought it was 2spot, she says / I thought he'd come back

—no / I was just, you know . . .

the bass at low body hum, still strapped around me / and the beats from the machine

—what did you see, elliot?

—in the liquid?

she nods

—I saw my mum and dad, making love

—oh

—they'd always told me this story / that they were there / and that it was there, that they / well / yer know / but I never quite believed / not till now

—do you think it's the truth, elliot / what's shown in the music?

—I don't know

she closes her eyes, just for a second

—he's not coming back, is he?

I look at her, for as long as it takes / and then say

—no / no, he's not

then she comes forwards / slowly, as though to . . .

as though to . . .

until she's so close, all I can see are the

amp-lights reflected in her eyes / and when she touches the bass with her belly, the tiny lamps in her eyes become a graph of the soft noise / and the wetness / so close we're almost kissing, and then . . .

and then we are

plug me in, two time

and did yer ever get kissed, I wonder / ever get
kissed so bad
did yer?
did the world slip away for a second / just there
as the lips touched your own / and the stickiness
clung / and did the stickiness cling in shreds / in
tiny shreds of spit that caught each on each / like
a sharing, like a secret, like a cradle?
like a cradle stretched as your mouths
separate, just for a moment / and then close
again / gathering the mucus / gathering the other
person's lips into your own / sealing the holes /
and the way the tongue of one touches the
tongue of the other, making a filament / like a
small lamp being lit in the mouth / a soft wet buzz
of electricity
did yer ever get that tingle going on in there /
did you?
and the sudden flood of the pink light, from the
tongues' contact / seeping upwards into the brain
/ and the way the dark flashes in your head just

then, the dance of the static / and the charge of it / the input and the output of it / and the charge of the kiss, slithering

did yer / did you ever get a kiss like that?

oh yeah, maybe you did / just about maybe and perhaps you did / but did you ever see all of it calibrated in your lover's eyes / caught, traced, calibrated and burnt / right there in the graphic fuckin' equaliser of your lover's eyes?

ah well then, you missed out

bass player's lament

every small moment of love has a concentrated tone / held special / filtered, purified,
and recorded for ever in the heart, which is the
night's black spool of tape

a strange love / never talked about, only done
/ never acknowledged, only performed / in the
moments suspended, here and there / and here
and there / and here / and there / as the night
stretched away, into morning / one night of a
passion sharp, muffled with a clenching hand /
and kept secret, even from ourselves / clan-
destine and stolen, even from ourselves / but
rich enough, for all that / certainly, rich enough for
me

because you know how it is, when it gets dark
/ how we find love where we find it

or else we lose it

or else never find it at all

the call

somewhere, a bell is tolling / high and shrill / it wakes me / the telephone / again, I'm surprised by donna's presence / all through the night, the skin's surprise, as I find her there, beside me / the sudden warmth

but now / this time, leave her to sleep / instead, let's see who this is / maybe it's 2spot / walk naked downstairs to the hallway / pick up the phone

it's the police / with a word that stops my heart, shuts down the brain / cold / and all through the talking, all I can think to ask is this

—how did he do it?

and yes / he cut his wrists in the bath / in a cheap hotel / and when I give the name of the hotel, the cop asks me how did I know that / and I say

—his grandad did the same / the same place

—oh, runs in the family does it?

which was a fuckin' cruel thing to say / but it doesn't seem that cruel / not just then

—yeah, something does, I answer / something sure does

I'm standing there, stark naked / shivering / just holding the phone in my hand, long after the cop has gone / long after / until something soft, something warm, brushes my leg

I slide to the floor, wrapping the cat in my arms / against the flesh / lying there / with the sweet deep engine of its purr close to my face / and nothing will come / no tears / no fuckin' tears will come / what's wrong / why won't any tears come out of me?

and then I have to go upstairs and tell the news to jody / and to donna / and I really don't think I can do that / I really don't

a note, a small envelope addressed simply

jody, elliot, donna

donna, donna, donna / this isn't serious, and nothing to do with you / some things just have to be done, and this is one of them

I know you won't understand / but understand this

I love you

jody, keep the van and the instruments and the amps and everything / do good stuff with them, and make sure the others know that a new drummer is a fine and necessary thing / don't be silly about this / and stop writing bloody songs about me

elliot / I hardly know you really, but it was good playing the rhythm together / but that's all gone now

2spot

Bass Instruction Manual

To wake the strings so tightly bound, let slide
The finger's nub along the neck from fret
To fret; from bridge to nut, the tones collide
And sound the joyous air! And yet, and yet . . .

If root of base desire the song deny,
In tempting play of lover's serenade;
No matter then how crafted skill apply:
Inside the heart remains a note mislaid.

And never truly voiced, the song's domain;
The chords a code as yet misunderstood,
When love is tuned against the vein's refrain
Of scratches and samples, the body and blood.

two

**vibegeist
(spirit of the groove)**

the new code

—who is it?

—elliot

—who is it?

—come on, elliot hill

—who is it?

—let me in / it's raining

—who is it?

—oh / the bass player

—who is it?

—jesus / I don't know

—who is it?

—I don't know / I don't know who the fuck it is!

and the door / the door slides open

studio ghosts

traces of a kiss, coming back to me as I'm watching donna sing / this dolled-up woman, all neat and layered hair and a tailored suit / what's happened / through the glass, a dark-eyed lens / but the mouth, and the way it moves, just so around the words / the silent words

things have changed / of course / of course they have / we all have

the mouth is the same

jody at my side, headphones on, working some controls / her changes, perhaps the strangest of all / less driven somehow, less fiery / and when she takes the phones off, her hair, her once-upon-a-time goddamn cut-to-zero hair sticks up in sharpened tufts

—funny, she says

—what is?

—funny, how she turned out

—yeah / suppose

the singer sees me then / it's a barely there

glance, and I guess she's nervous about the recording / I hope that's it

it's one year, just gone / and in all that time . . .

ah / leave it alone

—listen

jody works the desk, nudging a slider up a pathway / the vocals seep through, over the monitors / no music as yet, just the vocals / dis-embodied, floating

and then I know . . .

it's a crazy situation
to think our love mistaken,
to fly right off the handle
broken, stirred and shaken

. . . it's her

the melody edged with a soul that never quite reveals itself / so tantalising / and that was always the way with donna / always the way, even in real life

and yet, and yet / there's something missing from the voice

—it's the first time she's sung, says jody / you know, since we / since we split

—we didn't split, we just ran away

—you did, elliot / you ran away

I just look at jody / I really don't need this, and jody knows it

—sorry, she says / and thanks for coming / really

and like I said / where's the old mad, bad jody gone?

—well / I'm more surprised donna's here / than I am

—oh yeah / she's here / she's here / listen now, the chorus / just listen to it

spirit of the groove
turning like a ghost
inside the rhythm
of a love that's never given

—is that good, or what?

—well, yer know / let's hear the music

—she's married, did you know?

—she's what?

feeling sick / dizzy / the naked song reaching into me / throwing me away

—well, engaged / oh yeah / career, all that / computers / big money / engaged to a pro-grammer / a black guy / I guess she, yer know, went back / what's up / you ok?

—yeah . . . yeah / I'm fine / fine

jody shrugs / she doesn't know / she doesn't know what happened between donna and me, that night / that night that

ah shit

jody moves another slider / another / a whole

series of them / bringing in the music, track by track by track / first as a soft caress / and then further, louder now / locking tightly with the vocals

> *shaken, broke and stirred*
> *the music's never heard*
> *too late to disentangle*
> *I never knew you cared*

and I'm shocked / because, well / it's fuckin' brilliant / far more so than anything that glam damage ever managed / totally out there / a dance of the weird / no regular beat, but a kind of flow to it / intricate, sparkling, evolving / involving / dense layers of sound, folded into each other, confusing the feel / I hear guitars being played, soft and then jagged, and then a blurred mirror of noise / and the drums high in the mix / but whispering / whispering funk, close to the ear / and sunbursts of notes, electric chords / bangs and clatters / unknown noises / surges of distance, breathy / the glisten of wet strings, mixed into a shimmer of voice / somebody talking, dissolved, into nothing-ness / and donna, singing

she doesn't sing all the time / it's a long piece, seventeen-and-a-half minutes, jody tells me / and the vocals disturb the flow every so often, gently / just another layer in the mix / layers upon layers of sound / and yes, there is a ghost in there, turning / some other quality, a shiver of lost love, caught in the rhythm

spirit of the groove
living in the boombox
haunted by the sound
of a love that's never found

—this is our first single, jody says / *vibegeist*, we're calling it / well . . . ?

—yes

—you like it?

—yes / I do / it's good / it's very good / you did this all yourself?

—glued it together / it's all stolen of course, every last note / hundreds of samples /

—it's about 2spot, right?

jody shrugs

—in the letter . . .

—yeah, I know / don't write any more songs about me

—so?

—ah / come on / just this last time, ok / just to get me started again

—finish it off, yer mean?

—finish it off / whatever / yer want to start thinking about the bass?

—I don't get it / just sample the bass as well

—I can't do that

—why not / get bootsy to play it / or mingus /

bernie edwards, he'd be good on this / no, no /
robbie shakespeare / yeah, nick some shakespeare / perfect

but jody's shaking her head

—it's got to be you

—why?

—just listen to the drums

ok / it takes some listening / the beats are
stretched ragged / cut up / reassembled / pasted
/ wasted / brought back to a different kind of life /
but there it is / floating / lost

—it's 2spot, I say / you sampled 2spot?

jody nods

—that's why / that's why it has to be you / you
and donna

—shit

—so then?

—ah / I'm not sure

—look / one bass-line is all I'm asking / then yer
can go back to london / whatever / one crappy
bass-line / what do yer say / don't yer think 2spot
would want it?

—no / I don't think he would

there / said it / jody's face takes on a hard
aspect, just for a second / her eyes slit tight,
turning parched / then she closes them completely, lets out a long, long breath / and when
she opens up again, suddenly, she looks old,
beyond her years / and tired beyond the day

—you're letting me down?

—I'm a session man, jody

—good / treat it as such

—what's really going on here?

—what's really going on / is that I'm clean

—you're clean?

—six months now / six months / and I mean everything / everything / all gone

—well, that's / that's great / ah / forget I said that

—it's the music, now / it's just the music

and I remember 2spot saying more or less the same / all that time ago / all that time

—well done, jody / really

—damn right, well done / and listen close now / here we go

because donna has finished the last chorus / and there goes 2spot, playing those spirit cymbals, into the fade-out distance

—let's go in / come on

I follow jody through into the studio / and straight away, I see that she's living there / all her belongings piled on the small bed / down to this / and donna is saying she's sorry about the take, and that I distracted her, and jody says

—that's fine / you could try again, later maybe?

—yeah / later, maybe

and I'm thinking well that's nice / and then she turns to look at me

—well, elliot / what the fuck are you doing here?

said with just enough edge / and then

—I'll be upstairs

—yeah, says jody / that's great, donna / great vocals

—sure

and then she's gone / and jody says to me

—so / will yer do this?

—she hates me

—she doesn't hate you

—she does / I knew she would / I knew it

—look / just fuckin' play, will yer / lay some deepness down for me, elliot / the old deepness, eh?

downriver bass

here I am / all alone inside the headphones, and the rhythm starts to slide all around me / now that I know, and now that the music's close up, it just seems so exactly 2spot / all the rhythms / all the magic / captured precisely / feels like I'm falling into this stream of sound / going back and coming forward / backwards and forwards, caught on the wave of a wave

and now / my fingers / already moving over the thick, metal strings / I don't have to think about it / the strings play themselves / falling, falling . . .

I can't remember what they played, or how they played it, and afterwards, when jody flows it back to me, I'm amazed

because you do the pub circuit for too long, playing your standard rhythm and blues trash, it gets so you forget anything else

I mean, this is the first real stuff I've done in ages, in years / shit, let's get this out / it's the first good bass I've played since the damage / well, since the damage was done

say it, say it
the first good stuff since 2spot killed himself
and the other thing
well / it's obvious what's going on

a life in the samples

we play the *vibegeist* song back a few more times / jody messing with the levels and the mix of tracks / hands moving quickly over the board / playing the sliders / doing the dub

—so what made you do it?

—what?

—get clean

—well / yer know, after 2spot died . . .

and I'm thinking / oh, maybe I shouldn't have asked

—after 2spot went and fuckin' killed himself / and the band split up and all that shit that happened / well, I just went a bit daft, I suppose / yer know, how donna gave up the singing and got herself that computer job and the new bloke and all that / and you ran off to london / well that was you two going daft / but when jody goes daft, I mean she goes daft like serious / you know what I'm saying here, elliot?

—yeah, I know

—I had the opposite intention to you two / I was

going to go rock'n'roll ultimate / no way was that stupid fucker gonna stop me

—2spot?

—yeah, the stupid fucker / jesus, was I angry at him / so fuckin' angry you wouldn't believe it / so I just went mad / I thought, he's not gonna stop me, he's not

—what / another band?

—first off, yeah / but all I ever heard was crappy-arsed musicians, thinking they were the latest thing / they just didn't have that dazzle to them, yer know / so what was I supposed to do / piss my life away with the little boys, and the little guitars, and the tiny, tiny drums / well . . . no / so I fucked it over, and just went mad on myself, playing myself / man, I took some stuff, I tell you / doing the submerge, all the way

—you always did

—what, when I knew you / in the house / that wasn't drugs, that was just getting myself ready for the drugs / I still had a life then, I had the music / and that kept me connected / without the music, I just got myself cut off completely / I became this creature, this thing on the end of a dripfeed / I had next to no money, so I was doing some nasties to keep me in dirt / I won't go into it / fuck / I was the mother, I tell you / the mother of dirt, and you know the saddest thing / you wanna hear the saddest thing of all time / even at the bitch end of life, in the dark, in the shithole / I was still thinking it was rock'n'roll

jody breaks off for a second / listens to the *vibegeist* unfold / her eyes seem to be following every beat, every stray rhythm as they bounce around the board / she makes a fine adjustment to one of the faders

—jody?

—yeah?

—did you ever . . .

—go on / what?

—no / nothing

—did I ever think I was going to die / no / not ever

—why not?

—because of 2spot

she says this as though it's the most natural thing in the world

—right on the edge of me going too far, I would always get his face in my mind / and his rhythms, yer know / and they'd pull me back / pull me right back / oh shit / poor 2spot / we could've helped or something, I don't know / realised / we could've realised

—yeah / we could've realised

jody's tears / and silence / just listening together until the song comes to an end / and jody hitting the replay button, automatic

—that's great bass playing, elliot / it really is /

it's just what we need / listen to that!

    —so what then / you gave up / what, in a clinic?

    —no / on my own / I was so out of it, I'd lost the music / just thrown it all away / and then I got this idea / about using 2spot's rhythms / and that just seemed right, somehow / and something to aim for

    —something to get clean for?

she nods

    —and now what, you're living here?

    —just for the present / getting it back together, yer know, and working night and day on the new stuff / re-using the music / all those tracks we did / *scorched out*, and everything / all those practice tapes, they're all in there / I don't know, just making something good from them / is that stupid, or what / I mean, is it?

    —no / no it's not stupid / but why the globe?

    —what?

    —oh come on, jody / you can stop messing with those faders now / this is liquid music / yer didn't really think I wouldn't recognise it

    —well / it had to be, didn't it

she hits a switch / and the globe pops out of the desk / and when she hands it me, I'm scared / I'm scared the thing will burn me, or something

    —jody, this stuff is illegal now

    —yeah / and this is maybe the last machine in the country, I don't know

—you kept it back?

—I stole it

—the club knows?

—the club knows / 2spot's mum, she wants this to happen / some kind of memory / and yer know, we only have a few of the globes left / look / all we're doing is using the liquid to make the track / get it down on vinyl, and then that's it / all gone / finished with / do you see that?

—ok / I see it

—we have to make this track happen / it has to be brilliant / it has to / it has to tell the story / that's it / 2spot's story / everything / the reasons why

—the reasons?

—yeah / the whole thing, beginning to end

—you've put, what / his grandad's stuff in there?

—his grandad's / his dad's

—his dad's? jesus!

—it has to happen / look, I've made some tapes for you

she's reaching under the desk, pulling out a plastic carrier bag

—all the glamour stuff, the figs stuff / and this as well

she's handing me a cassette / scrawled on the case, these words

the glamour, 1977, unexploded blonde

—what is it?

—the glamour's last album, unreleased / demo tapes / I found it in 2spot's room / his grandad was working on this . . .

—the year he died?

—the day / the day he died / I thought you might want to listen / you want them?

—what for?

—to listen to, ya stupid fuck

at last / a glimpse of the old jody

haunted by the rhythm

I'm walking across the dancefloor, instrument case in one hand, the bag of tapes in the other / the floor's bright and shiny, freshly cleaned / the place real quiet, in that particular way that affects turned-off dancehalls / lonely, with the ghosts . . .

—elliot!

it's donna / she's walking across the floor towards me

—what's the idea? she asks / coming here like this

—jody asked me

—you shouldn't have come

—you came / you sang / what's wrong with you?

—that's for 2spot / I'm singing for 2spot / who are you playing for?

—playing for? I'm playing for . . .

—you're playing for yourself / always, always / always for yourself

—donna / this is stupid

—I detest you

—donna!

—I detest you / what's jody playing at / bringing us together, the same time / I asked her not to / fuck / what's she trying to do, get the group back together / oh / I shouldn't have come, I knew I shouldn't have

—but you did . . .

two people / two people, alone on a dancefloor / suddenly, not daring to look into each other's eyes

—I'm sorry

it's almost tender, the way she says it / almost

—I'm taking it out on you

gets me turned around, just a little / and what exactly am I doing here, anyway / why did I come back to manchester / it's not my home any more / it's just not my kind of place / any more

cold ghosts, hot ghosts, and crazy types

oh yeah, and I played a little bass one time / scratches and samples / dubbed, redubbed, mixed and fixed / samples of the heart, ripped out bloody, lost in the edit

shit

—I didn't know / really, donna / I mean, jody didn't say anything about 2spot, and the music and all that / it was just a job, she said / just a job

—just a job?

—I don't think I'd have come / if I'd known /

but now I've done it, while I was playing, I don't know / it suddenly seemed right / did you get that?

at last, she turns to look at me

—oh yeah / what's jody done, one more dance record, without a black sample / but that's manchester for yer / down on the people

—oh

because she's never talked about her race before / not ever

—I'm not joking, elliot / I really am very angry at you / shit / at myself

—I know, I know . . .

—you don't know / you just don't know

—it's a year ago, donna

—I don't care when it was / I've never forgotten him, not for one second

—and do you think I'm any different?

—you didn't even come to the funeral

—I couldn't have stood it

—now that really got to me, that did / told me what you were

—ok / ok, you're angry / ok . . .

—it's not that / it's just / I feel so . . .

—what?

—lonely

—lonely?

—so lonely / without him

—but . . .

—that's it

—jody said you were engaged / to be married

—I'm engaged / am I engaged / I am engaged, and mortgaged, and careered, right up to my neck, and rising, and soon I'm going to go under, and that's that / you heard me, I can't even sing any more / and do you think I'd be like this / if 2spot was alive, still alive / do you?

—oh donna . . .

—no / no, I wouldn't

—you can't know that

—I'd be dirty / and exciting / and full of whatever / of life / I'd be / I'd be beautiful

I shake my head, but what can I say / what the hell can I say?

—donna, you know I'm divorced now . . .

—shut up

—I'm just saying, that's all

—don't you know / I'll never forgive myself / for what happened that night

—donna . . .

—that night between us

all the pain she keeps there / in the words / if I could only respond / properly / tell her things / tell her how much I love her, really / tell her how much it means to me / but

—that's what killed him

—donna / that is just / that is just silly / we don't know why he did it / we don't know!

—we should've found him / helped him / gone looking for him
    —we didn't know
    —we didn't care / we didn't fuckin' care

the punk in the rain

I leave her there / alone under the lights / walk to the door, and press the exit button / the door slides open, the requisite five seconds / and as I'm leaving, somebody grabs me, trying to push me aside / we struggle for a moment, and then I fall onto the bass

—hey!

a man is trying to get into the club / but the door closes before he can manage it / and then he's just banging on the panel, shout-ing

—let me in!

—who is it? asks the door

—let me in, ya fucker!

—who is it?

I'm lying there, in the rain / just watching this man / his fists smashing again and again against the door

—who is it?

—deezil / let me in

—who is it?

—george axle, ya hear me / george fuckin' axle
/ let me in

—who is it?

—let me in / please / let me in

as the fight goes out of him / and he slips to the
ground beside me, crying

crying all these old punk tears / like the rain
that falls

the rain that falls

it just falls, and keeps on falling

vocal serenade

—that fuckin' bitch / that jody / she's using my music / ain't that so, eh?

—I don't know

—the fuck yer don't know / of course yer know / you're the what, the bass player?

—the bass player / elliot

—fuckin' bass players / I fuckin' hate them

—right

—you ever hear me sing, kid?

and what am I supposed to say / sure, I smoked some music, and went back in time, and saw you messing up at the electric circus?

—just the one song, I reply / from the first album

—and I'm good, right?

—well . . .

—ya fucker / what's wrong with you?

—it's just screaming, isn't it

—jesus fuck / it's punk rock / it's the bomb

we're sitting in a café called the 10cc, right there on happy mondays arcade / the place is a quarter-way full, and all the way dismal, with a smattering of low-lifes slumped over the plates of grease / an old slobber of a chef stirs the pans / the waitress has the same skin colour as the overcooked food she's carrying to the tables / while techzak music seeps like gravy from crackletown speakers / and opposite me

I can't believe it

2spot's father

a big guy, made out of brick / hands all cracked and dirty, the fingers buttered with nicotine / with tarnished hair the same colour, a slight recede shown off proudly / oh yeah, a real heavy presence / so downloaded, it's hard to imagine 2spot coming from the same code / sure the same blue-glint eyes / but these jewels set in a face of dug-out pits and crevices

—what the fuck yer looking at?

—nothing

—yer see these / these lines / there's one for every day inside / one for every day

he's making a jailhouse origami of a roll-up / sets the end of it on fire / sucks deep

—so / what's the game?

—what do you mean?

—what's with this recording I hear about / you're stealing my songs?

—some / I think so

—yeah well / that should be me singing up there / that should be me

—it is you

—yer what?

—it is you singing / it's a sample

—don't give me that sample shit / I fuckin' hate that shit / fuckin' dance music / what's that, like fingerpainting / oh look, oh look at me, I'm pressing a button / I'm a fuckin' genius, me

—it comes from punk, one way

—fuck off / it does not come from punk

—anyone can do it

—it comes from black music / from fuckin', stinkin' black music

jesus / what can I do / what have I walked into / and I realise that my head is shaking, side to side, with some kind of nervous fear

—ya no like the talking, eh / six years, kid / six fuckin' years, with bad behaviour / the full stretch

—I don't know what you want

—sure you do / some payback / some money

—I can't

—can't?

—can't help you

—I don't want any fuckin' help / I just want some goddamn respect

—you think you deserve it?

—ya what?

—I'm saying . . .

—what the fuck are ya saying?

—your son . . .

—my what?

—2spot . . .

—what of him / eh / what the fuck of him?

—ah . . .

—where ya going?

—home

—home? where the fuck's that?

—london

—london / oh, I don't think so

he's got me by the arm, pulling me back

—look, kid / elliot / sit down / ok, I'm being too nasty / will you sit the fuck down!

I sit down

—ok / I'm pissing off the bridge / sorry / let's get us another tea, eh / hey, doll!

he's shouting over to the waitress

—over here / another two teas / sharpish

the man stubs out his cig / starts another / working automatic

—the thing is, kid, and I'll freely admit this / I'm a hard case / I was hard when I went inside, and it just made me worse / shit / I'm forty-six this year / where's the life gone, eh / where the fuck has it gone / sure, I've done some stupid things, and enjoyed them, but somewhere in here, twisted, black and stumped, who cares, there's something that just about feels / just about / do you understand what I'm saying / do you?

—yes

—do you / in here?

he's banging a fist against his chest

—something / in here

—in your heart

—my what?

—look, george . . .

—who / listen / don't call me that / the name's deezil

—deezil . . .

—last of the true-faith punks, eh / oh, cheers, love!

the waitress places the teas on the table

—what it is, ya see / the old man called me georgie / the bastard / I mean, can you credit that / george fuckin' derek / I mean, what kind of name is that for a true-faith punk, eh?

—ok / deezil . . .

—yeah, last of the true faithers / damn right

—why do you hate 2spot?

—eh?

—your own son . . .

—he's the one with the hate / he's the one

—it doesn't bother you, that he killed himself?

—of course it fuckin' bothers me / what yer saying?

—and your father / you're surrounded by suicides

—I'm too strong, me / it won't get me / I won't let it get me

—what is it?

—it's the demon / the fuckin' demon

—the demon . . .

—sure, the manchester demon / don't yer know, kid, it's suicide city / top of the charts / listen to the music we make / and not just us / I mean all the music / all the fuckin' manchester music / you never heard joy division, what's wrong with you / the smiths, the fall / it's a dark-side party

—dance music isn't like that

—yer what?

—joy division became new order / dance music / it's all about life, isn't it / all about being, yer know, alive

—you fuckin' twat

—right / so / what then / you're blaming the city / the music?

he looks away, just for a second / the first sign of doubt

—you got a dad, have you / a mum?

—one of each

—and you get on do you?

—ok

—well / now there's something / ok / ok's good, isn't it / oh yeah / the ok family / hello, we're the ok family / we don't have any trouble / no trouble /

no trouble at all, ok is / as boring as fuck, ok is / don't you agree / I mean, don't you just wish sometimes that you could take your dad by the scruff of the neck and say, fuck off! fuck right off, you twatting bastard / I bet you'd love to do that, wouldn't you / eh, just sometimes / well, wouldn't you?

   —yeah / yeah, I would / just sometimes

   —but you see, with 2spot and me, it wasn't like that / it wasn't ok / it just never was ok

   —why not?

   —well, look at me

I look / and he looks back at me looking / and I look at him looking back at me looking

   —yer see it?

   —I see it

   —I know yer see it / because you've got it as well

   —what?

   —it's right there, kid / right in the eyes / yer just can't love, can yer / no matter how yer try / no matter how / yer just can't get it right

   —that's not true / I . . .

   —it's fuckin' luminous on ya!

he smiles / a twisted grin / and I ask, right into it

   —did you hit him?

   —hit him / of course I fuckin' hit him / didn't I tell you, I'm a crazy fucker

—he was . . . he was hurt / very hurt, I think / but like, secretly / he kept it all in

—oh / there wasn't much hope, with 2spot and me / none at all / especially after he turned out that way

—which way?

—which way / you knew him well, did you?

—no / only for a couple of months

—a couple of months / well, fuck me / a regular 2spot expert

—I liked him

—I'll bet you did

—he was / he was a good . . .

—a good what / a good fuck?

—a good drummer

—oh yeah / now there's something / a good drummer / listen, kid / there ain't no such thing as a good drummer / no such thing / all drummers are arseholes / and listen, I should know / I've beaten up enough of them / curse of the planet, they are / the fuckin' curse

—your own son . . .

—getting his own back, wasn't he / I mean, all that puffed up rigmarole / all that prancing about / what was all that about, eh / how he turned out / dressing up, like that / playing the pansy / now there's a slap in the teeth / to a man like me

—what are you saying?

—he was a fruit / he was fuckin' gay / oh come on, yer must've got that?

—I . . . I wasn't sure

—not sure? the bastard used to wear make-up / oh yeah, age of six, I caught him / just staring at that fuckin' sleeve / and smearing all this stuff, his mum's stuff / all over his face

—which sleeve, a record sleeve?

—his grandad's record / the fuckin' glamour / what kind of name is that, for a band

—no / he was playing, that's all / playing games / he loved his grandad

—loved him? he never even met him / the old geezer topped himself years before

—I know that / I found that out / but he said / he said his grandad taught him everything

—oh sure / the kid was mad for the geezer / playing those fuckin' albums all the time / and he was only six, seven, when he got into it / jesus / what a waste / it's me he should've loved / me / his fuckin' dad / and I wouldn't mind, but I tried to get him listening to the figs, yer know / he wouldn't have it, the stuck-up twat / and all that fairy music

—fairy music?

—I mean, what's the point of punk, if it's not to kill that shit

—2spot had a girlfriend

—oh sure, he told me that / some black girl / as if

—he told you?

—sure he did

—but you were in prison

—yeah, and he'd come visit me / what / what's up / is there a problem?

—no / I . . . I just didn't think . . .

—well, he did / near every month

oh, now / let's see this / all those times that 2spot took off / is this what he was doing / visiting prison / and every time he came back, so donna said, he'd have cut himself again / new scars / new wounds to the body

—what did you talk about?

—you know the funniest thing / it's just about the closest we ever were, me behind bars and all / it is fuckin' funny that, don't you think?

—I suppose so

—and the funniest of all / he spent all the time talking about how much he hated me

—because you hit him?

—don't be fuckin' stupid / he liked being hit / the kid was born to be hit / no / not that / the thing is, yer see, those last times / those last times he visited me, just as I was getting ready for my release / well / he'd really got the idea from somewhere, that I was responsible

—responsible?

—for his grandad's death

—and were you?

—no I was not / but the kid had grabbed hold of the idea / and that's all that mattered

—ok / I see that

—but yer know, it's good isn't it / that he hated me / because that's not ok, is it / because that's not the dreaded ok / because what's that thing you mentioned / that machine?

—machine?

—that fuckin' machine you mentioned

he's banging his chest again

—a heart / you mean the heart?

—yeah, a fuckin' heart / you need a heart, to hate / don't you?

—yeah / you do

—so then / 2spot had a heart / he had a heart for me

—if you say so

—I do say so / and that's why

—why what?

—oh yeah / now there's love for ya

—love?

—yer don't get it, do yer

—get what / get what?

—why the lad killed himself / yer just don't fuckin' get it

—I'm trying to . . .

—jesus christ / you're worse than I am

rhythms of the city

and that's it, the guy tells me to piss off / and I'm glad to / out into the rain, coming down full strength now / fifteen minutes' slow-driving, to get to the hotel / some mock-gothic monstrosity, the best in town, right there on simply red street / a nice room, for a week / all expenses paid by the zuum people / a week, for fuck's sake / in manchester / what's to do in a week?

trouble is, the idea of just going up to the room, well . . .

if I'm gonna be lonely, I'll be my own kind of lonely

so I get out of the car, walk round to the boot / I'm drenched through just getting there / open it up, and there's the bass / and behind it, the carrier bag / the tapes . . .

in the driving seat, looking through them / everything's here, the whole story / the 4 glamorous men, the glamourboys, the glamour / the three figs albums / and also

a globe . . .

what's that doing here / jody must've thought I'd want a copy / the label reads

vibegeist mix #3

ok / let's hear some, for real

I put the first glamourboy tape in the car's player / start up the engine / start up the music / start up the driving, driving, driving

come on, manchester / play me some fuckin' bass!

all around the centre, listening to the *ready steady skiffle!* music / just riding the beat along / reacquainting / circling around something that isn't quite there / getting lost in the one-way systems, and all the singing street names

joy division terrace / rick astley street / sad café drive

soaking up the music, and the rain's percussion / some people are out, so used to getting wet, they don't notice hardly / sunday shopping, using up the weekend

john cooper clarke street / magazine boulevard / bee gees avenue

and here's me, hitting the fast forward every so often / skipping the moments, letting the tape turn over, play out, slotting home another

down oasis lane / around billy j kramer circus / along the hollies road

sometimes just finding a space to park in / some place that reminds me of something

and then driving, drifting, arriving, deriving /
songlines and dreamings

the fall parkway / a street called gerald /
glamourboys parade

what's that / I stop the car, turn off the tape,
climb out / start walking

it's a little street, edge of the centre / no one
around / a few shops, some of them boarded up
/ well yer know, at least the group got a street
name / and then I see the sign, the blue plaque
stuck on the wall of a run-down building

*on this site 1955–1968 the famous 2spot coffee
bar and night club*

below the sign, a door / an open door,
unmarked / stairs, leading me down

at first, I think I've stepped into some sub-
terranean television showroom / all tuned to the
underwater channel / big fat colours pop and
wave / tiny little flickers dart, iridescent / the
world's a black pit, filled with globules, ship-
wrecks, lichen and slugs

it's an aquarium / a giant aquarium / a few
solitary men stand around, here and there,
inspecting the swimmers, making notes in little
black books / holding on to these bulging plastic
bags, full up with greasy water and the golden
goodies / I walk through the aisles, mesmerised /
round a large open pond, where giant specimens
swim through green water / until, at the back of

the shop, a forlorn middle-aged man stands behind a counter / head down in some obscure fishkeeping fanzine, but still keen enough to notice my arrival

—is sir looking for anything in particular?

—erm / yeah / kind of . . .

—we have more stock, in the back / specialist items / if sir would like to . . .

—didn't this use to be a club?

—a club?

—yeah, the 2spot / a nightclub?

—was it?

—there's a plaque outside

—look, mister / you want some fish, or what?

I leave him to it

back on the road again, letting the rain fall / and listening / passing landmarks, youthful things / getting a sandwich, eating it in the car / listening, following

stone roses junction / victor brox house / northern uproar cul-de-sac

I see a newsagent's / buy myself an A-Z of the city / check the index / there's a glamour walkway listed, right along the river bank / but no mention of the figs / there's a john the postman yard / a frank sidebottom villas / a biting tongues playground / but no figs street / no figs road / not even a figs passage / george axle, a man without a place

new fast automatic daffodil street / m people

mews / inspiral carpet warehouse

heading out of town eventually / down new order road / down to the strange, finding the old house / glam damage house / what is that, a new paint job, frilly curtains / I get out of the car / looks like any normal family home / and I know jody and donna moved out some time ago

gives me a shiver, just being there

the curtains twitch / somebody's looking at me

so then, back to the car, more listening / tape after tape / music, unfolding, losing me, finding me / I don't know where I'm up to / losing track / the music getting looser, more relaxed / becoming too much, too much to listen to / what's wrong with me / it's just pop music / just the usual cheap salvation of the pop dream life

durutti court / morrissey gardens / alberto y los trios paranoias roundabout

along all the roads, the rhythms play

glamology / just this one family, going through all the phases / growing older with it, from rock'n'roll to beat, to psychedelia, to rock, to punk, and beyond / fifties to sixties to seventies / beyond / me, skipping forward, jump-cutting / getting the picture all in one place / trying to, anyway / following through the twisted moments

genetic harmonies / disharmonies

a damageography

and then, suddenly, I know where I'm heading

rhythms of the blood

danny axle / with the 4 glamorous men

1957 *ready steady skiffle!*

1959 *live at the 2spot*

with the glamourboys

1963 *postergirls*

1965 *embrace you*

1968 *swirl*

with the glamour

1970 *damaged goods*

1973 *tainted vein*

1977 *unexploded blonde* (unreleased)

george derek axle / aka deezil / with the figs

1977 *skull*

1979 *flesh*

1981 *vapour*

william axle / aka 2spot / with glam damage

2002 *scorched out for love*

and now?

2003 *vibegeist*

how far, how far?

sometimes, she listens

away from the centre, mile after mile of the tapes unwinding / doing the history / thinking about what donna said before / a white-boy history / past the church of take that / the slaughter dog hotel / the glories of the black grape carpark

oh / now just wait / what was`that?

I turn the car around, park it in front of the hotel / just this seedy two-storey building, nothing good to show for itself / and yet / right here / danny axle did the deed / and then 2spot followed him / slaughter dog hotel / jesus, they should have a sign / suicides, special rate

time to get going, I think / and the further you drive down the old smiths road, one by one the musical names start to disappear / so by the time I'm moving through weaver street, coal street, engineer street, with the rain finally giving it up, I know I'm home

home?

the mam's on me, straight through the door / giving it all the

—oh, look at him / oh, look at him, dave! look at the boy!

tears, already / laughing and crying

—he never lets us see him / never lets us see him / it's a shame, it's a real shame, it is / never lets us see him, not at all he doesn't

you see what it is with the mam / tears and joy, there's no barrier between them / heart to brain, direct fuse

—oh, look at him, dave! a year he's been gone already, and just look at him!

whereas, with the dad, no fuse at all these days / there he is now, hanging back, trying to work out a suitable expression to wear / shaking my hand like I'm a door-to-door salesman

—and he never even said goodbye, says the mam / off to london, he is / and never even saying goodbye

so I get to eat the biggest meal I've had in years / receiving all the updates on all the people I can hardly even remember any more / from what I can gather, most of my old friends still live around here / mam's insisting I go look them all up, but I can't think of anything more hideous / meanwhile, the only thing the dad says in all this

—lovely roast, susan

—just the one glass of wine, dave / remember?

what's happened to him? and when will it happen to me / when will the fires burn out / and maybe they have already, playing the crappy r'n'b in the pubs of london / and if they're burnt out already, when did it start / when did the fires get rained on / with 2spot killing himself / or with me getting into the drug thing / or before that / years before / when I was just a kid, trying to keep out of the dad's way, the dad's drunken way / or else it started the day I was born, to such a tight household / or before that even / just being got like that, made like that, fucked into being like that, in the carpark of a lousy broken-down punk club / was that the spark of me, or the snuffing out of me

perhaps I was infected by the music that night / maybe they bred it into me, the punk trash conception

and then I'm looking over at the dad, thinking about the bass strings / those stupid strings he sent me / sent in secret / maybe that was the bad start of me / all my stupid life coming from that gift / and why did he do that

he's looking at me / he's looking at me / and then looking away

ah, he was better drunk

after the meal, we sit around / we sit around and sit around / long lost and never found / we sit around / until the mam says to the dad

—well, david / talk to him, talk to him

and he says

—still playing that bass, are you?

—yes, dad / still playing that bass

and that's it / the mam starts crying, from nowhere

—oh that poor man / that poor, poor man!

—what have I said? says the dad

—that poor mister 2spot!

now then, she never met him, not the once / it's just what he represents, that brings the tears / all the dirty roads I've gone down / the rock'n'roll business, the drugs and everything / the drinking / the suicide, the running away / I know she thinks I'm as bad as life gets, I just know she does / and can I prove otherwise?

—that poor, poor man

and the dad says

—now then / let's not get into all that

oh yeah / we're an ok family, no problem / we've got ok up the arse

as I'm getting ready to leave, the mam rummages in the antique record player, and pulls out nothing else but a copy of s*corched out for love*, twelve-inch vinyl

—I listen, she says / just sometimes

groove cutter

here we go now / there's a few things in the hotel, a spare shirt, some toiletries / let the staff have them / and the bill, let zuum sort it / I'm out of here, direct route / bypassing manchester / I'm through, basically / done the bass, done the tour, done the mum and dad / 2spot's dad, jesus / enough / finished / the circle road, catching the motorway going south

south / away / gone

playing the last of the tapes along the way / the final shine of the glamour / twilight falling, the perfect time to catch this music / you know those moments, when a tortured saxophone sobs like butter / and the voices cloud the mix, darkening a smile / it's that song again, the one 2spot played me / so proud of what his grandad was doing / so proud / the veins tainted with poison

what the light considers
the dark of moon delivers

and shit, yer know / it comes to me / maybe I'm wrong / maybe it's not about drugs at all / maybe, just maybe / it's about having a child / a kid / a bad kid, gone wild / the tainted vein

the sun that burns on midnight's turn
devours and spits and shivers

and maybe, just maybe, it's not the sun that burns, it's the son / it's about father and son / the father and the son, and the hatred between them / no, no / listen close / it's about how to live / how to live with yourself, after you've created something bad / a child that's bad / a child that hates you / that devours and spits and shivers you / a bad kid who calls himself deezil, just to spite you / christ, what the hell's going on with this family?

I have one glamour tape left / the unreleased demos for the 1977 album / *unexploded blonde*, the title / and at first I think jody's made a mistake, given me the wrong cassette or something / because it's dance music, more or less / just these swathes of soft noise / a bare rhythm / isolated bass / mechanical drums / cold, distorted voices / jesus, old danny axle was pushing it some / and then I think of the whole german scene, and the stuff bowie was doing at the time / and how white boys finally got hold of dub reggae / giving space to the music guess what / it's fuckin' brilliant!

and then I think of 2spot, in the middle of this / what was it like, being brought up by deezil / how did he survive for so long / by falling in love with the grandfather, of course, the dead grandfather he never knew / falling in love, through the music / the old vinyl groove escape route / making it real / what was it 2spot said that time?

he made this music / it'll live for ever, and now it's all mine

christ / so lonely / and all that cool he had, just a frozen heart, maybe / kept in check, because otherwise . . .

what sent him over, I wonder / over the edge into actually killing himself?

something in the music, perhaps / the liquid trip we made / something in that last argument with deezil / the last *imagined* argument at the electric circus

his anger / 2spot's anger, when he came down from the trip / and the running away

I try to imagine the moments / the slow, dark moments that pass / knowing that his father's going to be released soon / burning with the hate, and then / some final moment of release, perhaps / thinking, perhaps, to escape the poison / the poison in the blood

that question he asked, just before we took the first liquid smoke trip *do you believe that every human being has the right to damage themselves*

and the stupid answers I gave back

shit / and then 2spot killing himself / escaping the bloodstream / drowning himself

revelations of the autopsy / the final cutting of that mapped-out flesh / that the water in the bathtub had taken him, before the veins had emptied / a portable river / the freezing cold portable river of the night

the manchester night, where the demon lives / is that the way it was?

somebody tell me please

because also in the body, they found traces of some unidentified substance / a song, in the bloodstream

is that the way it was?

fall down in secret places

where am I / where I am / lost in the music

a slow rain against the windscreen brings me around / making a blur of the car in front / sudden swerve, and pull back / easy does it / I've been driving on auto / so I

and then I

ah, right / it's not raining, is it / it's me / it's the rain in the eyes, only

shit

I pull off the motorway at the next exit / get myself parked / I'm in some hideous non-place / some lonely stretch of the night / plastic cash-and-carry warehouses and featureless, window-less engineering works / there's not a human being in sight / oh lord / I'm sitting in a beat-up car, in a beat-up world, listening to some off-planet music, and I'm sobbing / I mean, the tears are pouring out of me / great surges of pain, of deep hidden emotions, finally let loose

how long has it taken?

twelve months / twelve bloody months / what

the fuck is wrong with me / and maybe deezil is right

you just can't love, can you, no matter how you try

oh donna / donna, donna, donna

it's not 2spot / it's not him I'm crying about, not really / it's donna / the living / the best chance I had in a long time, to get the heart melted / the very best chance . . .

I let the album play out, getting submerged by it, and then finally start to relax as the silence takes over / just the whirring of the tape, as it continues through the machine / running into darkness / and I'm thinking, ah, there's still something on there, maybe a ghost of a previous recording / a distant bass, faraway drums, and the voices, I can almost hear them / it's got me messing with the tone and balance controls, trying to isolate the source / but then the tape reaches the end of the spool

click

and the voices are still there / I'm sure they are / still whispering

I take out the *vibegeist* globe / feeling stupid, I put the thing against my ear, shake it around / there's nothing inside of course, no sounds, but the voices in my head are suddenly louder, suddenly clearer

I was too young to know, and all the lonely

tears, fall down in secret places . . .

what is that / I know those words / I know them from somewhere / where is it?

one of those glamourboy songs / I cried my heart out over you / I heard it this morning, driving around town / and now I'm singing it to myself

the globe in my hands / vibegeist, dubgeist

everything's in here, the whole story / isn't that what jody said?

which means all I have to do is listen

listen deep

I start the car, find the way back to the motorway / the opposite route, back towards manchester / oh yeah, because it's not over yet, 2spot / I can't let it go that easily / I need to get back to the hotel, do some digging, some searching / maybe talk to your dad one more time / I need to find out why / why you lay down in dirty water and opened your veins / really / just to find some peace for myself

and a space / maybe, just maybe / a space to let donna back in

entering the city, I let the figs play loud, filling the car with noise / a manic attack, cleaning all other songs from the skull / punk's demon knife of love

as the globe tingles on the dash, with every passing headlight

liquid beats, blood music / samples of the

way back / samples and scratches, a life mapped out in vinyl / groove spirit / ah 2spot / at least you knew / where you were coming from

feels like I'm being dragged downstream, every mile I drive along

and the first thing I do, back in the room, is take the old magic bass strings out of my bag / and the second thing I do, is raid the minibar

it's my first drink in months

the night caller

when I'm called, I don't know where I am / don't even know who I am, not for a few seconds / until the room sways into place / becomes something / hot, damp sheets all wrapped around me / wine, beer and whisky, dried solid in the channels / slow through the brain, the wave- lengths of pain / like a beam of light, revolving / close-up, miles away / close-up, miles away / and then realising, ah, it's not the light, it's the sound

sound of the telephone / reaching out for it in the pitch dark

—elliot!

—uh?

—elliot, please . . .

—jody?

—help me!

—what / what's happened?

—it's donna / she's gone under

—she's what?

—it's donna / she's gone under / she's gone under!

slowly / slowly now / working it out

—elliot? you there / are you there?

—yeah / yeah, I'm here / look, keep calm / I'll come over

—oh please, hurry up / bring the globe / the vibe

—the what?

—bring it!

needle in the groove

—who is it?

—elliot

the door opens, first time, just like that / the rain hardly touches me

inside, it's like a graveyard club / the hush of the machines, all turned to standby / all the lights, turned to darkness / walk through, slowly / every single line of force concentrated, right to the dancefloor, exact centre / where the night seems darkest, alive with secret rhythms / it moves, the centre moves . . .

gallagher

I follow the cat, downstairs, along the corridors / past the kitchen, along to where the wooden door leads to the studio / down another level / the studio door / through / control booth / the window / through there, a dim-lit scene / jody looking right at me, her face split by shadows

the cat walks through the final doorway, and I follow it / all the way to where donna lies on the bed / the cat jumps onto her stomach, quite gently / I bend down, take her hand

—donna?

her sleepy face stirs at my voice / the eyes are closed, softly closed, and the trace of a smile plays around the lips / I stand up, turn to jody

—where's the ambulance?

—no ambulances

—what?

—no, we promised

—promised? jody, she needs help, proper help

—no, she said no / I gave her my word

—what is this?

—I gave her my word

jody looks distraught, tired / all the promises made, draining the flesh

—ok, ok / let's sort this / you gave her the stuff, did yer?

jody nods / holds up an empty *vibegeist* globe

—how much?

—all of it

—all of it? jesus / all that smoke? no way, she'd choke on it

—no, not the smoke

—she drank it?

—injected

—the needle? holy shit!

—elliot, she wanted it / brought the gear over herself

—and you agreed to this?

—she said / she said . . .

—yes?

—she said she wanted to find 2spot

I look down at donna / well, there's no pain, that's for sure / not yet, anyway / I reach down, to stroke the tattoo on her arm / the 2spot / oh but girl, what kinda love you been keeping / what kinda heart you possessing, it can take you this far?

—how long's she been under?

—oh / some time . . .

—how long?

—an hour

—right / that's it / I'm calling them

—elliot, no . . .

—where's the phone?

—it won't do any good

—jody, I'm doing it / don't try and stop me

—the door / they won't get through the door

—give them a password

—I've jammed it / straight after you came through / jammed the programme

—jody / it could damage her!

—where's the globe / you brought the globe?

—what's going on?

—give it to me

—why?

—give it to me

so / I hand over the globe / *vibegeist mix #3*

—there's only this one left now / donna took one / the other's the master / this is it

she's turning the globe, around and around in her hands / and from the look on her face, the sudden fix . . .

—jody . . .

—there's no other option / I've gotta go in

—don't be fuckin' silly / come here

—don't try and stop me, elliot / I'm going in after her

she goes over to the bed, sits on it, right next to donna's legs / I watch her doing all this, it's like I'm watching a film or something / a slow-motion study of the ways of the world / watching, as jody picks something up off the floor / a plastic bag / inside, a number of syringes / watching, as she chooses one, cracks the wrapper on it / next, she breaks the seal on the *vibegeist* globe, sticks the needle into the valve, pulls up the plunger

the syringe slowly fills, turns blue / a small collection of the sky

a well-practised hand gets rid of air bubbles / a thin trickle of the music, spilling over / and then the tying of a ribbon, around the upper arm / pulled tight with the teeth and the free hand / until the veins enlarge, stand proud

—jody . . .

—it's too late

—I'm thinking of you / I'm thinking of you, breaking the habit / don't do it / please don't do it / the needle, jody / it'll just drag you back

—I'll take the chance

the ribbon, unleashed / the tip of the needle, pressed against the flesh

—stop!

I go over, grab the syringe from her

—elliot!

—fuck it!

I stamp my foot on the other syringes, the ones in the package

—what are you doing?

—stopping you coming after me

—what?

—give me the ribbon

she does it / gives me everything I need / as I pull her off the bed, take her place / the cat's purring beside me, curled up on donna's thighs

—but you're the same, says jody

—no, I've been clean for years / more control

—elliot . . .

—ok / ok / ah / who the fuck am I kidding / the thing is, jody, well / I love her

—yeah / I know

—donna / donna needs to know

oh shit / the way I remember precisely how to use the ribbon / frightening / how to get the veins up and ready / how to angle the needle just so, 45 degrees to the bloodstream

I look at the studio clock / it reads 4.06am

—give me fifteen minutes / if we're not out by then, call the ambulance / you got that / you'll promise me that?

jody nods

needle kiss the skin / pushed home / and then, thumb to the . . .

—remember, says jody / it's a different mix / you'll have to search around

—ok

the cat moves against me, as I press down on the plunger / jam that spike

home / burning

plug me in, vibegeist overload

did yer ever get drugged / did yer / did yer ever get drugged and popped, and danced and kissed / and did yer get the heartbuzz, the bloodsonic drugbeat of a dancing pop kiss / and these kisses, were they like drug percussion kisses / like electric popdance frequencies / like insect chimes / like a drugsoft shimmer / a kisspop and drumkiss liquid bass affair / and did yer ever kiss a drug, pop a drug and dance a drug / did yer / did yer ever do that, so far, it's like a boombox rendezvous / like a blood mix / where the beat is always one groove away from the needle's end / clouds of dance coming in, clouds of sparkle, kissing the drums / and did your bass ever get cloud-captured, made soft, with all the notes veinshot / climbing the mix, in orbital rhythms / something to float away on, in the waves of noise from the speakers / and then finally, falling / and in the fall, did yer hear the voices / like a drumvoice, distant, almost on the very edge of the edit / and was it the whispering dub, the murmuring /

the long lost and never found / the voice you've been almost just about hearing all your life / the four-string ghost / finally, finally played upon

did that kinda thing ever happen to you?

did yer get yourself some drug / like I got me some drug / got me some popkissdancing drug, all the way burnt / with the four strings, catching fire, one by one

until

blood sample 57

one string / they only gave me the one string to play with / just this wooden box, a broom handle and a piece of goddamn string / string, real string / I'm supposed to make music from this / left hand desperate to find a place on the handle / the right plucking madly at the jive / ok, call it a rhythm, stick to that / make a breakdown stomp for the singer to raise a shout along

johnny o johnny o
johnny o'palaver
born with the devil may care

match the guy beside me, scraping raw notes from a pigskin banjo / and the guy behind, scratching those thimbles over the washboard / and danny the man up front, swinging that guitar / one real mess of a sound / but yer know, it's rocking / we got a stewball going on / here's where I come in, finding the harmonies . . .

went out a sporting, ended up courting
the devil's fiery glare
ohh
the devil's fiery glare

made it / made it just fine, all the words coming to me / and down / keeping it going, and getting into it / as some kids down the front start to dance / it's a complicated movement, the girls with their swirling skirts / the lads all dressed as we are / check shirts, blue jeans, soft shoes / ill-lit stage, bare stone walls, cheap equipment / behind me, strung across a wall, a torn-up sheet / oh yeah, I made it this morning, wrote it by hand

rocking the 2spot
danny axle and the glamorous men

oh yeah, oh yeah / I'm a glamorous man / try and stop me / making the one-string bass talk like a fullthroat / jazzing the changes / no electricity, just the box to amplify me / but loud, loud, loud / ragged and proud / making a merge with the drums and the board / with the feet of the dancers, spinning around / and all the kids along the sides, moving their hands in the new jive code / hot / sweat on the walls of a downtown cellar / all the clatter and bang of the rattle and twang / one last string run, down to the tonic

then we're done / last song of the set / the

crowd make a noise for us, and it feels so good /
this could be my life, maybe / making music / just
sitting there on the edge of the stage, talking to
the girls / danny beside me / I have to keep close
to this man / he can write the songs / don't know
anybody else who does that

    —good stuff, guy, he says to me

    —sure thing, diggin' it

    —what were you playing there?

    —oh, yer know / some new lines I worked out

    —yeah well / keep it nasty, guy / keep it sweet

    —sure / sweet and nasty

    somebody's slipped a coin into the jukebox /
don't you rock me daddy-o, by the stretford
blades

    —ah / someone's got a joke on 'em

    the blades are the next best skiffle band
around here / a long way the next best

    —square time / at least nobody's dancing

    now we're sitting in a corner, round a chipped
table / sipping at frothy coffees / a young woman
joins us / danny's wife / he puts his hand on her
stomach

    —what's in there? he asks

    —danny!

    —that's my boy in there, he says to me / my
little boy

    —you don't know it's a boy, says his wife

    —of course it's a boy / can feel him kicking

—don't be silly / he's not kicking yet / he's only just started

—feel that rhythm on him / oh yeah, the georgie boy / gonna be a player

around the booth where we're sitting, a cut-glass mirror / my face comes back to me, fragmented / my hair, combed back immaculate / I push my hand through the thick, greasy wedge of it, loving the feel

—hey guy / we got the business here

two black men have come up to our table / airforce uniforms / danny's looking over the gear they've brought

—oh yeah / we dig this / bassman, ya see this / *brooklyn stomp*, the 1932 version / we'll have that, most definitely / and what's this?

—rhythm and blues, man

—ah, I don't know / guy, do we dig this?

—let's see

I take a look at the record / *hoochie coochie man*, by muddy waters

—yeah, dig it / this is the one

—you sure / I mean, it's not our style

—we can change it around / maybe get ourselves plugged in

—sure / change it around / guy's also saying that / ok, what do you want for it?

so, we make the deal / all records bought come out of the group takings

—now then, says danny / there's some taste

because now the jukebox is playing *solid gone sweetheart*, the b-side of our single / and the kids come out to dance / I love this / watching people move around to the stuff we do / it's the life / and that gets me scared, just thinking about my eighteenth birthday coming up soon

—danny, I don't wanna go away

—ah, it's only two years / if I can make it, you'll make it

—but ya know what I'm thinking / I'll do the service, come back / you'll have a new bassman

—hey guy / listen to me / we'll keep it hot for ya

the tight, cramped floor is packed now / a twist of colour / dazzle and spice / something in the air I can't quite place / a tingle / aroma / ah, now then / I look over at the two airmen / will I look that good in a uniform, I wonder / with their midnight faces focused on something elsewhere / like a distant, darker planet / and I follow their eyes, all the way / right to the centre of the floor

where two people dance

two kids, just dancing the night away / one white, the other black / a boy and a girl / and the tingle comes back to me, informed by a scent of flowers / and a car starting

lavender / lavender, petroleum / hair grease

2spot!

2spot and donna / doing the diamond jive

and all the days, the weeks, the years come zooming / gathering around me / what's happening / and what I am doing here / the name's not guy / the name is elliot / elliot hill / I play the bass / the four-stringed bass!

—guy! guy, where yer going?

—later, danny / later

through the dancers / transfixed, as the boy flings the black girl around / catching the tails of themselves, every last second / centrifugal / and then, saying the word

—2spot . . .

the dance breaks in two

—what?

it's the girl / it's donna, looking at me / the fear, the fear on her face

—no! 2spot! wait!

the boy's running now, through the crowd / to where the stairs lead upwards, outwards, along / and the girl, she turns to me, close / angry

—donna, I never . . .

she's gone, and I'm running after her / climbing the stairs, feeling jumpcut crazy / taking me outside / cold, bitter / manchester / the moon a full peach of a thing / golden, shining on the cheap, painted frontage of the 2spot coffee bar

donna's standing alone / on the small back street of nowhere

—I was dancing / I was dancing with him!

a certain lingering scent in the air / dispersed /
filtered clean / and when I look at the moon again,
I see now I was mistaken / it's the smallest
possible crescent

the city darkens around me

—donna / come back with me / donna?

oh / she must've slipped away somehow / she
must have . . .

and when I turn to face the coffee bar, I
see that the sign has changed / cleaner, brighter,
louder

the 2spot nightclub

a neon two of hearts, burning, on and off / on
and off

and a different music plays from within

I go through the door, buy a ticket / and then
start down the stairs

blood sample 64

jammed / tight and shiny / tight, shiny and dark / I'm dressed in the latest / three-button tailored, single vent / sharp on the collar / three-tone cloth with the sparkles, all gold and green and purple / slim jim tie, with the pin / and the fringe travelling, down to the eye / every day, further down towards the eyeline / I'm gonna shine / who's listening / tonight, I'm just gonna shine myself a beam / force a way through the crowd-stream / hand in the pocket, deep in the crush / fingers closing around the pills, the tiny travellers / keep it cool, for the fools / head down, hand up, slip the benny in the lips / feeling the charge, as the beat gets louder / moving now, just moving, through the darkness and the smoke / towards the stage / the burst of heat, and the surge of the blues / the hoochie coochie mojo man, blowing the mike / sky high

the glamourboys

tight and shiny / tight, shiny and dark / with a feedback spark / waves of applause / no pause /

riding the feeling, straight into the next number /
this ballad / the springs and twists and turns of
melody, precise, like a knife across the heart / all
about how the singer cried his fucking heart out /
and all the lonely tears, yer know what, they fall
down in secret places

yeah, right

the round the way fans, with the out of tune
tears / for all the crazed and fiery nights spent
down in this cellar / for all the songs they think
belong to them / to them alone / tried and tested,
down in the dark, the shared dark

push through, further, closer to the stage / it's
so easy, moving like this / even with the tightly
packed bodies all around me, I move like smoke
/ must be the tablets, getting me slippy / through,
to where all the girls enjoy / the squash / the
reaching out, reaching out for the singer's legs

—danny! they scream / danny, danny!

all the dreams of the city / contained within this
one band

looking past the singer now / between the
bass player and the lead guitarist / through, to
where the drummer brings the skin alive / he's
good / they said he was good / and he is good /
too good / too good for this band, or any band /
he's playing rhythms like they haven't invented
yet / holding back from the beat / holding,
releasing / until you just can't stop moving to it

you just can't stop moving

2spot, they call him / bloody silly thing, isn't it / calling yourself after a club

the girl I'm looking for, she's right there at the front / the black girl / the only black girl in the place / I tap her on the shoulder and she turns / gives me a bad look but what the hell / I grab her hand and start to pull

the girl struggles / maybe she even screams / all lost in the noise and the crowd / and I really think I'm doing this / the whole club's starting to dissolve around me / the music, losing its beat / pulling / pulling the girl away from there and back to

—get the hell off her

a sudden blow / spins me around

the drummer / the drummer's on me / the smell of him / the sheer lavender fucking smell of him / the petrol of him / it all comes flooding into my brain / and I know / and I know, even as the rest of the glamourboys pile in, dragging me down / under / the wet, sticky floor / hard blows / kicks from pointed heels / stamping on my hands / bringing the damage

and I know, even in the darkness / I've lost the tune again

hey! dj groove selector / bring another mix on

and then the lights catch fire / and flower

blood sample 68

so, ya know, man / ya know what's happening / well, danny boy / yer know danny, from the glamourboys / well they did this gig in london, and met some cats / and danny comes back home with this drip-drip / sure, baby, a whole bottle of the fix / and he gives me a drop / one drop, two drops / right there on the blotter / he says, take these tonight, come down the club, watch us play / it's the last night ever / so yeah, I put myself on it, man, take the skull burn / get down there / ya know the place, the two of hearts / a real swirltown happening / night of the shutdown / all these colours climbing the walls, sliding around / and I get a colour, stuck in my eye / the colour turquoise, like a splash of blue tears / there's not too many cats there / plenty of room to move, real slow through the rhythms, crawling from the speakers / a screaming, rolling special / voices of children / *the clocks go blind, the days unwind,* oh yeah / it's like I took my head for a swim / downstream, downstream / hair hanging, over the eyes / feeling loose, in every step I take / flared / sucked into the music / caught in the bass-line / endless, endless / and at the end of every note, donna rides, donna rides, always one note ahead of me / amid kaleidoscope flowers / donna, I say / words like glue on the tongue / donna, donna, donna / come back with me, come back with me / grabbing a-hold of her dress / donna, leave him be / leave the drummer be / just saying it over and over, until she slips away / slips away / slips away / *all the jokes, are told in smoke*, and as the place floods with liquid, I get the taste of the rhythm, on the eardrum / aroma / flowers / petrol / and then the flowers fall, one by one / donna, will you marry me / donna, will you / and the line of petrol catches fire / *whoosh!* my hair's on fire / in the funny little town of swirl, my fucking hair's on fire, man

blood sample 73

it's cold, tonight / so cold / I'm standing outside a club, over the other side of town / it's a stylish venue, strictly smart attire / now look / you see this jaunty number / the cashmere coat, the grey suit and tie / and the wife at my side / the beautiful wife, dressed in her best frock / oh yes, we'll do / the saloon car is parked, safe / and we have tickets / we have everything we need / everything

all this week at swaggers cabaret bar
supper dance with
hit sixties singing sensations
the glamour

excellent / inside, all the tables are laid out, just so / candles, wine baskets / oh, it's very up-market / very discreet / oh yes, they put on a good show, at the swaggers / I lead my charming wife to our allocated table, and as I do so, she says

—can we not move closer to the stage?

—now don't fret yourself, donna / these are our seats

—oh but, elliot . . .

—we can enjoy ourselves, perfectly well from here / perfectly well

we get a few looks, of course / but we're quite used to that by now / after all, we have the same standards as the rest of the clientele / we eat the same fancy meal, with the same delicate manners / and the band come on stage exactly as we're finishing our dessert, perfect timing

oh, I remember them well, the glamour / of course, back then they were known as the glamourboys / we heard them quite often, my wife and I, and in some dreadful dives, let me tell you / still, we were young then / so very young / and it's nice, isn't it, to hear the old songs again / of course, it's not the original group / not all the original members, I mean / but the singer's the same, and that's all that matters, isn't it? and they do all the old favourites

I cried my heart out over you, oh now there's a song / why don't they write songs like that any more / it means so much to people, so very much / and donna, donna is singing along, just to herself of course, one shouldn't make a scene / and shall we dance / yes, let us dance / on to the floor, arm in arm / around and around / with more couples joining us, all lit with the sparkle of the mirrorball / shots of light, scattering

it's cold, tonight / so very cold

we dance closer to the stage / and closer still / why, it's almost as if my wife wants to show herself off, to the musicians / really, I do have to keep my eye on her / well, one never knows, does one, with her kind / really, perhaps we shouldn't have come here tonight / and once safely back at our table, I say to her

—now, what was all that about / showing yourself off like that?

—oh / it was a long, long time ago

—what was?

—a long, long time ago / I'm not sure . . .

her gaze is drifting, over towards the stage / as if drawn / closer, closer still / to where the singer stands, speaking to us

—here's a song from the new album / one for the boy / wherever he is

what the night uncovers
within the heart of lovers
the sun that's torn on twilight's dawn
snaps and cracks and smothers

now then / what's this noise / that's not a tune / that is not a tune / and those words, where is the love / where is all the love we were promised / and all around, from table to table, the diners start to chatter / louder, louder / the singer carries on / and the more you look, and the further he sings / see now, how strange he looks / why, the man isn't even dressed properly / shaking, like he has a disease / and what's that on his face, make-up / the clientele are restless / and would rather talk, and order more drinks, than listen to this, to this . . .

—look, says my wife / look, the drummer . . .

the young man has risen from the drumkit / he grabs the microphone from the singer

—you lot, he says / you lot, you should be listening to this

—how rude, says a man at the next table

—you should be listening!

it's cold, tonight / so very cold, outside the swaggers dancing and entertainment club / and a grey, downhearted rain begins to fall / dissolving / the band are loading their equipment into a van / the single word there on the side, *glamour*, and the word *boys*, painted over

donna insists we pay our compliments / she walks over to where the drummer and the singer stand alone

—I liked your show

the singer looks up / plainly seen, behind the smeared mascara, all the broken dreams

—thank you, he says

I touch my wife on the shoulder

—come on, dear / we have to go now

—just a moment

she turns to face the drummer / something

passes between them / some feeling I can hardly
dare fathom

    —haven't we met before? she asks

    —yes

his single word / my wife is set alight

    —I knew it / I knew we had / but where . . .

the drummer smiles at her / devastating

    —come on now donna, I say / we really should
be getting along / the babysitter . . .

    —no / you go / go on without me / I want to stay
a while

    and like the fool that I am, I turn and walk
back towards the car / our lovely saloon / feeling
myself, melting / melting away in the rain / the
boomsonic rain

    it's cold tonight, isn't it / so very, very cold

scorched out for love, dubgeist remix

scratching mad magic
splinters and tactics
scraped from the shimmer
of samples and static
boomsonic boomsonic
kaleidofunkphonic
let the vinyl glide

finger drag scatter
pop rattle and clatter
the rhythm's incision
twindeck precision
boomsonic boomsonic
kaleidofunkphonic
let the vinyl glide

grooving 'n' smoking
bass-lines invoking
turntables revolving
in crackles dissolving
boomsonic boomsonic
kaleidofunkphonic
let the vinyl glide

blood sample 77

a bass guitar / plugged into the sun
let the vinyl glide
and I shall play this number, speeding / through
a line of flow, of fire / of speed / through a line of
burning speed shall I flower / four lines, of burning
speed / faster, faster, screams the singer / and I
shall give my body up to the final bass, the burning
bass / it's a punk flame that I seek / yea, even amid
the howls and the scratches / and the one million
samples of a life lived, and lost, in music

lived, loved, and lost / spat upon, shat rapid like
blades from a flower

good times! bad times! good times! bad times!

it all comes down to this / that when I open my
eyes, I'm on stage at the electric circus club /
manchester / and now I know, that this is my
place / born to be here / and all down the line, to
this stage, this wash of filthy light / this cage of
crackle / here I am / a dark mass that pumps the
noise, a surge of hair and bone and flesh / and

three simple chords / three simple chords encase me / four strings enwire me / three hundred souls surround me / I'm a slave to the tune, the beat, the group, the jeers of the crowd

I'm the mule / holy fuck, I'm the bass player with the figs / the fuckin' figs crew / arse band of the universe, and I'm loving every single moment / every single pumpshit nowhere moment / with harmonies of saliva, watch me

even the good times turn out bad!
even the good times turn out bad!

behind me plays mondo, on the drums / beside me fluxus, on the guitar / ahead of me / deezil, setting his tongue on fire

bad bad bad!

and this time, I know everything / why I'm here, and how I got here / the liquid mix / looking out now, into the crowd, and seeing donna there / out there, with her arms around 2spot / and thinking, right, that's it / enough / getting this sudden thing, this urge, as the crowd start to curse and throw things / to just pull off the bass / take a screaming run towards the moment where the stage ends / and just to leap

to leap, into the noise down there / sailing towards where

into the crowd / arms waiting, to beat me / and

bloody well kill me / just trying to get through to donna / one last time

frozen, caught in flight, above the pogo / and

let the vinyl glide

you'll find me in the gents, taking a piss / surrounded by chaos graffiti / all the lousy bands who ever played the hole and never came back out / and catching myself in the mirror / its black depths far worse than the bunged-up toilet / my face reflected, cracked in pieces, crowned with spikes / christ I look bad, hardly there / a skin of flickers, eyes of glaze

I have this picture, this captured moment in the glass / and when I turn round

let the vinyl glide

and when I turn around, I'm suicidal / just floating through the air once more / slowly / stage-diving, into the crowd / arms reaching up to grab me / and stop me / from just getting through, one last time / to where donna stands / and

let the vinyl glide

—where is he?

—uh?

he must be the oldest person here tonight / some crazed nutter

—you're the bass player, aren't you?

—yeah, but . . .

—where's georgie?

—georgie?

—deezil / where's deezil?

shit / it's danny axle / thin biscuit hair / jagged bones / eyes in a mantra / strung out wild

—where's my son?

vinyl glide

time's getting twisted / around and around the groove / falling now, slowly, slowly / through the noise, into the arms of the crowd / ah shit, if I could just get through to donna / just the once before the needle jumps / shit!

vinyl gliding

all the way backstage

—what the fuck is this? says deezil

—my latest stuff

—pops, yer all fucked up

deezil puts his arms around some major punk girl

—listen to it

danny axle has brought a small, cheap cassette machine with him / a wire stretched from it, to a pair of plug-in earphones / he's holding this line out to deezil

—jesus, what is it with you?

—unexploded blonde

—yer what?

—my latest stuff / please / I did it for you

—oh fuck off

I'm watching all this from a corner of the

dressing room / the air stinks like an armpit / punk musicians wander through, sit around / one guy lying flat out on the floor / just sweating up the place / somebody's spray-painting a large letter T on the wall

—listen to it, please / just listen

—I'm busy

deezil grabs the girl hard, takes a nasty kiss, right off her lips

—listen to it

—christ almighty

deezil snatches the wire, plugs his ears with the music / and he's just laughing

—fuckin' jurassic, pops / jurassic and a half

—you're not listening

—it's over, dad / we don't need yer any more

he knocks the machine to the floor / brings a doc marten down on it / the look on danny axle's face / the blankness written there / and beyond that, through the doorway, I see 2spot, watching / watching all this / watching / and as I move towards him, following the sudden scent / the flowers / ah

vinyl on the glide

and don't yer know / it's a slo-mo heart that can fly like this, right over the crowd's desire / and then, twisting / coming down / losing height / a snatching hand grabs me / pulls / pulls at me hard / oh please, mr dj, let the groove become a wave *and let the vinyl glide me, slowly now, so slowly* . . .

finally / outside / cold wind, and a touch of rain / and I remember, the last time I was here, it wasn't raining / I wonder which is true, which remix / some kid, painting TIME'S UP on the wall of the circus / a bottle falls from a top-storey flat / falls, and smashes / I walk towards the carpark / over there, my father's car / I remember, I remember . . .

the rain falling heavier now / and standing beyond the car, two men / 2spot and the grand-father / 2spot and danny, their arms around each other / something is said, and then the grand-father moves away / the rain takes him

I wait a while, and then walk over to 2spot / flowers / flowers and petrol, overwhelming the air / supernatural / he turns at my approach

—mr bassman / how yer doing?

—ok / and you?

—oh, yer know / he's gone / that's the thing

—your grandad?

—every time / every single time, he has to go to that bloody hotel

—you keep coming back here?

—oh sure / playing the same old tune, over and over / just trying to get through to him / trying to make him listen

—trying to, what / persuade him to stay?

—why / why won't he listen / why?

he looks away briefly / after the figure depart-
ing

—I died with it, didn't I / died with the tune
inside me

—scorched out for love

—totally scorched / and now he's gonna kill
himself / over and over, in that bathtub / that
bloody hotel . . . jesus / if I could only . . .

it rains / and keeps on raining

—2spot?

—yeah?

—I've come for donna

—ah / that's up to her

—let her go

—what?

—she's not singing any more / let her go

he looks at me / a deep, straight look / and
then he smiles / and says

—I promised deezil / that I'd murder him, once
he got out of prison

—oh / right

—there was no turning back on it / you do see
that / no turning back

—yeah, I see that / but you couldn't do it / so /
so you killed yourself instead / is that it / what /
some kind of fear / some kind of guilt / is that it /
2spot / tell me / come on / I need to know

he smiles once more / and then lets it die on

his lips / then he takes me by the arm, and leads
me around the carpark, towards the back of the
circus / a beat-up van is parked there, the single
word *figs* on the side / and waiting beside it, is my
father / my young punk of a father

　—dad . . .

yeah, I actually say it / and the young punk
turns to look at me / that faint glimmer of recog-
nition passes / and then a sadness prevails

　—yer know, says 2spot / there's a thing between us

he's steering me gently, towards the van

　—between us / what do you mean?

　—take a look

he opens the backdoor of the van / and inside . . .

a genuine punk love song, vibegeist remix

now then / here's a story

sunday oct 2, 1977, the last night of the circus / fused / sparkers of the flame / and all the manchester bands playing over the weekend / the remembered and the dust

and the fans / place them up there with the players / the wall to wall mess of people

but move in close on just two in that audience / nobody famous / a man, and a woman / call them that, a boy and a girl really / teenagers / little punks / but the boy was on the scene, trying to be anyway / knew some of the bands, just to talk to / and for this special night, he'd invited the girl along / it was only their third date

but still / something got them going that night, something wicked / and white hot sulphursonic / this super fast whine of guitar and twine, dragging a tide in their blood

their names are dave and sue / just ordinary names / nothing special except / that afterwards, around the back of the building, in the rain, the boy was persuaded / made stupid / cold, left out and stupid / he did it / yer know, let his girl go loose, all for a touch of the rock'n'roll dark / like bending down to pick up a diamond, and ending up with your hand in the dogshit, the smelly, sticky lump of it / as he let his girl go with the singer / in the lousy beat-up van, with the singer

and that, as they say, was my mum and dad, doing it / deezil and sue / and what they were doing, the dirty, that was me being made

once upon a time, a child of the buzzcocks / now, a child of the figs

ah fuck

ah fuck, ah fuck, ah fuck / as I push myself away from the sight

falling . . .

slaughter dog hotel

falling, through the air / into the crowd / arms grabbing at me, pulling me down / and suddenly, I'm fuelled by something, something hot / something that tells me I can do this / I can move myself through the music, no trouble / right to where donna stands / just learning to ride the waves of the sound, at last / making like a dj, working the spike through the grooves of black life / I'm the man, the man, the needle-fuckin' man!

kid liquid / just turning the circles

and then the crowd have me / closing around me / tightening / pulling me under, further / and down / and further down / below the low and deepcore / black vinyl gliding me / melting the noise and the lights and the crowd / clean away

ah / so peaceful

just this vast expanse of deep blue liquid that I'm swimming through, naked, alone / music is playing, somewhere far away / oh so very far away / but that's ok, all I have to do, now and for ever, is float around in here / in the deep blue loving stillness

and never feel anything / not ever, not ever

not ever not ever not ever not ever / with no music to plague me

with no music, not ever / oh, but only . . .

only, that tune being played / oh so very far away / calling, calling

upwards / upwards, towards the light / the swirls of red

and through / gasping for air as I come up / breaking the surface of the world, the thin stretched melody of the world / playing so close, and only for me / only for me

I was too young to know
how to fall in love with love
but I cried my heart out over you

I'm lying in a dirty bathtub, filled with dirty water / streams of dark red liquid extend from my wrists / oh, they must have holes in the skin, to let the red stuff get loose / how strange

I force myself into a kneeling position / look over the rim of the tub, and there's a lonely boombox / playing the lonely tune

and all the lonely tears
fall down in secret places
when I cry my heart out over you

and sitting beside the machine, this black cat's looking at me / one good eye, set tight upon my naked flesh

jesus, it's cold all of a sudden / I'm shivering / get me out of here

so I stand up, as best I can / feeling weak somehow / and catching a glimpse of myself in the mirror, the peeling mirror

I have 2spot's face

and looking down

I have 2spot's body / 2spot's arms / the muscles like wire that once worked the drums / and 2spot's hands, that once twirled the sticks around / and his wrists / the two open gashes, one in each / the blood still flowing

oh shit

oh god / oh my god / please / jesus / help me / please / somebody fuckin' help me

I stumble towards the bathroom door, bang it open / tumble through / just this terrible, cheap hotel room / stained wallpaper, unmade bed, the smell of the used-up life

and then I'm falling, all the force gone from my bones / hitting the carpet / down flat

broken

from where I'm lying, I can see the telephone / bedside table / I start to crawl towards it

—you looking for something?

I jerk my head around

—well?

It's deezil / lounging in the armchair / I didn't see him / why didn't I see him?

—help me . . .

—what / what's that / sorry, I can't hear you, son

and I want to tell him, I'm not your son, I'm not 2spot / my name is . . . my name is / but the words won't come, and the room is blurred / I reach out towards the phone

—oh, you wanna make a call?

I start crawling / but deezil stands up, comes over to me / he sits down on the floor, cross-legged / right in front of my face

—you see the thing is, son / it's a bit late / it's a bit fucking late!

then he drags me, just pulls me right across his legs

—that's right / come to daddy / lie down across daddy's lap / just like the old days, eh / just like the days

he's stroking my hair, my wet hair

—this didn't have to happen, yer know / it really didn't / we could've sorted it / we could have / what do yer reckon / shall we start again / shall we make amends / uh / shall we / just throw it all away / and start again

I want to tell him to fuck off / really / really I do

with a stupid old cat staring right at me

and then the blood drains away completely /
taking my breath with it / and I let it all go
dying / right there in a cheap hotel room / right
there
in my father's arms

the last sample

—wake up / elliot, come on

—what?

—you're back

—donna?

—yeah, it's me / I'm fine / come on

—oh god / I thought I'd . . .

I sit up, wipe my face / it's covered in sweat / look around / studio zuum / donna beside me / and the cat sitting on one of the amps / no sign of the dj

—where's jody?

—never mind jody / look who's here

—yer wanna put that track on, bassman?

It's 2spot / he's sitting behind the kit, combing his hair / left side, right side / the quiff

—what . . .

—shit, yeah, says donna / let's do it

—one last time, says the drummer / set it rolling

—elliot . . .

donna's looking at me

—will yer work it?

without even thinking, I go into the control booth / fixing the globe to get the vibegeist flowing / the music starts

and straight away, 2spot starts to play along

to play and to play / real simple / just the extra beats where you least expect them / playing along with the samples of himself / making it real

so much so that donna just can't stop singing along / going up to the nearest mic, putting in the harmonies

I'm watching all this through the glass / too scared to even consider / that this man, this player / he's my brother / half-brother / whatever / my brother . . .

until in the end nothing at all can stop me from walking through into the studio / the cat slithering around my ankles / and then plugging myself into the bass / just letting the feel of it take me / along the congregation of these four bits of stretched, tightly pliable wire

spirit of the groove
fading in the mix
evaporating process
surrendering caress

and I know that when this song is ended / donna will have to choose / finally

between the drums / and the bass

the dancer

coming round, the first thing I do is check the studio clock / it reads 4.16 / I've been inside for just ten minutes / feels like my skull is filled with rhythm

—you ok? asks jody

—sure / I'm living it

—jesus / what happened?

—yer don't know?

—how should I know / I never took the stuff

donna's still there, deep down and drifting / the cat still asleep on her lap

—what's wrong? asks jody / didn't you find her?

well / what can I say?

—ah, it's up to her now / if she wants to come out

—so / ah, what now / we call somebody?

—listen / do yer have the *vibegeist* globe / the master?

—oh sure / it's in the machine

—play it, will yer / and get it down on tape / no, don't touch / just play it

so / jody works the desk, and the music comes alive / and the singing, the singing is harmonised / the drums are god-like funky / and the bass, the bass . . .

—bloody hell, elliot / I never heard you play like that, not ever / did the fluid do that?

—I guess so

—never heard it do that before / not ever

—turn it up, jody / turn it right up

turn it up loud, so loud / that donna just has to come alive / start to dance / open her eyes

come on girl / open up those moonlit eyes

Bass Instruction Manual

To wake the strings so tightly bound, let slide
The finger's nub along the neck from fret
To fret; from bridge to nut, the tones collide
And sound the joyous air! And yet, and yet . . .

If root of base desire the song deny,
In tempting play of lover's serenade;
No matter then how crafted skill apply:
Inside the heart remains a note mislaid.

And never truly voiced, the song's domain;
The chords a code as yet misunderstood,
When love is tuned against the vein's refrain
Of scratches and samples, the body and blood.

Until at last the player finds within
The key to which all notes a secret part
Ascending make; and there beneath the skin
Surrendering, a remix of the heart.

G D A E

and all the things I saw / and all the songs I heard . . .

later that day, I'm sitting on my hotel bed, dry in the mouth, heavy in the head / really, I could do with another drink, but yer know / I have to start again now / start again to learn how not to be addicted

but 2spot's dad / was he really there at the end, helping his son to die / and what the hell, he's my dad as well / is that true / is deezil really my father / all that anger he showed me in the café / did he know . . .

it's right there, kid, right in the eyes – yer just can't love – no matter how yer try, no matter how – yer just can't get it right

and then me trying to tell him that wasn't true / and him saying

it's fuckin' luminous on ya!

and how am I supposed to handle that / what do I do, ask my dad, I mean david hill / and my mum, ask them both what happened / dave and sue / what really happened, that last night at the circus / and where the fuck is all the love you promised me?

can I dare to do that / dare to ask?

and is that why 2spot couldn't kill deezil / because he's my father as well?

oh jesus / 2spot, 2spot / making all those murderous promises with the soul / and then finding them disallowed / but knowing inside, nothing's going to stop you, nothing at all / you'll do it anyway / kill the bastard / unless, unless . . .

the only way out / the drummer on the mix, taking out the bad note / and is that the reason 2spot killed himself / in order not to kill my father?

is that what the music's telling me?

and anyhow, it was all just another remix, wasn't it / of course it was / I mean, in one version of the song, I was married to donna / remember that / and that's not true, so why should this version be true / why should it mean, really, that deezil is the man?

only . . .

I have the old bass strings alongside me / all four of them laid out on the candlewick

the four strings I received as a kid / the G, the D, the A and the E

but / well, the E string, I bought that myself didn't I / and my name is elliot

Elliot

you see what I'm saying?
so then / the G, the D and the A
received, in that order
you see what I'm saying here / george derek
axle
George Deezil Axle
I don't know / I just don't know
I really don't fuckin' know
ah / what the hell

connecting

—dad?

—who is this?

—it's me

—who?

—elliot

—oh / right / I'll get your mother

—dad, listen . . .

—elliot / it's very late

—yeah, I know / I know that / but just listen a minute

—what do you want?

—oh, just to, yer know / just to talk

—to what?

—dad / you brought me up, didn't you?

—what are you saying?

—I mean / you brought me up and everything, right?

—of course I brought you up / all the good it did

—yeah, I know . . .

—the way you turned out, and all

—oh yeah / the way I turned out / that's right
—son / what's going on / are you all right?
—I'm fine, dad / just about fine

glamourboys parade

—you're sure this is the place? says jody

—this is it / there's the plaque

—ah, that's rock shit, that plaque system / they just stick them anywhere

—no / I was here / donna?

—yeah . . .

she looks around, away from the building / and I know that, like me, she's remembering back to that night / the night we stood here, outside the 2spot coffee bar / 1957, watching the moon change shape

—yeah / this is the place

—come on then, says jody / let's get it over with

she walks down the dingy stairway, and donna follows / and I follow, last of all

it's difficult to gauge donna's mood / it's the first time we've seen her, since the comedown, and even now, days later, she has a distance around her / as though some part of her, some tiny part, is still travelling the samples / down to the beat of the bone / I can only hope that what we're about to do . . .

—bloody hell!

it's jody, doing her reaction to the darkness / and the rectangles of luminous colour that stain the cellar walls

—will yer look at those fish!

—jody . . .

—but look at them!

—jody / keep the voice down

because the people in here, the customers and the man behind the counter, they're all looking over at us / and no wonder / donna and jody are the only women in the place / and already a few of the lonely guys head for the stairs / guilty / guilty of something strange

—this is it, right here, says donna

she's pointing at the large pool in the centre of the room / where golden bulbous beauties flick and dart / flick and dart / flick and dart

—this is it, this is it

donna sits on the edge of the pool, trailing a hand in the water / and remembering perhaps, how she and 2spot had jived the skiffle beat / around this very centre

—you after something? asks the man behind the counter

—just looking, says jody

she sits down beside donna / and I sit

opposite, keeping an eye on the owner / waiting /
waiting until he's serving a customer / and then
saying

—ok

and donna takes out the globe

the seal of which is already broken / only a
piece of sticking plaster keeps the liquid inside /
and then donna rips this off, puts her thumb
over the hole / turns the globe upside down, right
there, suspended above the pool

—elliot, says jody / yer know, it's the last
one

—look / we got it on vinyl, ok

—well yeah / but I still think you're crazy / both
of yer / crazy fuckers

—donna . . .

and donna slides her thumb away

the liquid falls, gently, into the pool / turquoise
/ turquoise music, mixing easily with the green of
the water / a fish comes to inspect the arrival,
thinking it food / nibbles / and then flicks away /
and flicks away / the glamour fish / and donna
whispers

—bye, 2spot

and I whisper something of my own, even
quieter / and I just know that jody's eyes are
rolling, but so what / she'll be thinking something
more or less the same / something more or less
exactly the same

—hey, you kids! shouts the owner / what yer playing at?

—nothing, boss, says jody / nothing at all

and then we head up the stairs / and out, into the cold parched sunlight of manchester

in silence for a while / each with our own / until jody says

—yer know, elliot / that guy's been asking for you

—what's that?

—that deezil guy

—oh yeah?

—sure / he's been ringing the club about you / wants to see you

—right

—so / what do I tell him?

—tell him / tell him, maybe

—maybe?

—no / no, tell him this / tell him that elliot says / repeat after me / elliot says . . .

—elliot says . . .

—elliot says, fuck off / say it, say it

—elliot says fuck off

—elliot says fuck off, fuck right off / say it

—elliot says fuck off, fuck right off / that's it?

—elliot says fuck off, fuck right off, you twatting bastard

—elliot says fuck off, fuck right off, you twatting bastard / that's it?

—that's it

—well, that's gonna make him happy

—yeah / the funny thing is / it will do / it will make him happy

and a little way further on, donna says

—do you think that we'll ever get a street name?

—what / a glam damage street?

—oh, we could, says jody / if we make enough records

—sure, says donna / we'll do that / but yer know, what if, like, all of life is just one big remix / what then / I mean, what if we're still caught up in it?

—ah, well then, I answer . . .

—ah well then, says jody / you'll need a bloody good dj, won't you?

and there they go / watch them / the singer, the dj, and the bass player / watch them / with the bass player taking the singer's hand

watch them / walking

away from a club called the 2spot

along glamourboys parade